THE GREATEST GRESHAM

Gillian Avery was the winner of the 1972 Guardian award, and was short-listed for the Carnegie Medal in that year.

'In this, a stylish and sympathetic comedy about two families of children living in a respectable South London suburb in 1891, the author once again shows her unusual gift for drawing on the manners of the late Victorian scene as if she were writing from the time. A splendid story.' *New Statesman*

Miss Avery 'is arguably the finest writer of domestic comedy for children today.'
School Librarian

'She is . . . brilliant, witty and spicy. She . . . shows heart and depth.'
Noel Streatfeild

Other titles in Lions

and many more

Gillian Avery

THE GREATEST GRESHAM

Illustrated by John Verney

COLLINS · LIONS

First published 1962 by William Collins Sons and Co Ltd
14 St James's Place, London sw1
First published in Lions 1972
Second Impression April 1974

Printed in Great Britain
by William Collins Sons and Co Ltd, Glasgow

Contents

CHAPTER I

The Coming of the Holts

The Gresham children were, so their father continually assured them, heirs to a great name. It was up to them, he would add, to do something about it and add honour to the name of Gresham; future generations looked to them. But he never told them what they should do, and on the occasions when these pronouncements were made (it was usually over the Sunday dinner-table because this was one of the few meals of the week that he was able to take with the children), Henry would look uneasily at his plate feeling that it was probably a reproach because he had not eaten the fat off his mutton, while Amy, the youngest of the family, would sit calm and impassive. She had a great gift for letting things that people said flow past her; besides, she was not in the least troubled by the responsibility of upholding the Gresham name, it never occurred to her that there was any difficulty in it at all.

But Julia thought about it a great deal. She was the oldest of the family, twelve. It was not the Gresham name that interested her so much as the burning desire to be famous and great in her own right, though she did not know in the least how to set about it. She would pore over the various books of biography that had been given to her, *The Girlhood of Famous Women*, *Famous Girls*, and the like, to see whether the lives of any of them resembled her own. What worried her more than anything was that most of them—except heroines, like Grace Darling—seemed to have shown signs of what they were going to be good at by the time they were twelve, and so far she had not decided at all how she was going to achieve greatness.

Charlotte Brontë, for instance, had been writing long romances and inventing a whole set of imaginary characters when she was far younger, but the only thing Julia had ever written was her diary (which she very often forgot to keep up for weeks on end), and various unfinished stories about a girl called Juliet who was very rich, very clever, very good and an orphan. She would also examine her face closely in the glass and search for signs of distinction. But she could not flatter herself that she found any. She had long thick fair hair, tied behind with a blue ribbon. It was really the best thing about her, she thought, because apart from that she had a large, rather plump, pale face, and very short-sighted eyes, so that her head always seemed to be poked forward, peering to make things out.

Another thing that troubled her was the very ordinary nature of her family; people seemed to do so much better if they came from an unusual background or had to struggle against immense odds. The Greshams were neither very rich nor very poor, they lived in a London suburb, in a house like hundreds of others, and Captain Gresham went into the City every day to work. The City was, as he frequently told his children, an honourable profession, but not one that he would have dreamt of himself had not circumstances dictated it. (This meant that Colonel Gresham, his father, had died leaving very little money and Captain Gresham could no longer afford to stay in the army.) However, he was determined that Henry should be a soldier, because it was the family tradition, even if it meant pinching and squeezing to save money now.

Julia, when she had considered all the things that seemed to be against her greatness, usually became very depressed, picked up the nearest book to hand, and after about three minutes would sink so deep in it that she would forget all her troubles. This is what had happened on a rainy September morning in the year 1891, soon after the Greshams had come back from their summer holidays by the sea. Their mother was out, and they had gone into the dining-room because Amy had said there was a removal van standing outside the next-door house.

'I haven't seen any furniture going in yet,' Henry announced. 'Just boxes, and they must be terribly heavy, the men are staggering like anything.'

But nobody answered him. Amy was too engrossed in watching the road. Being only eight she was unembarrassed by thoughts of being seen watching, and stood right in the middle of the window, pressing her nose to the pane and licking the glass, while Henry, two years older and rather timid by nature, crouched at the side peering round the brown plush curtains. Julia was reading, and paying no attention to anyone. She sprawled over the leather seat of one of the chairs that were ranged against the walls as if they were going to dance a quadrille and then, finding it at last too uncomfortable, slithered off and continued her reading on her knees and elbows on the hearthrug. Amy turned to look at her.

'Julia,' she said primly, 'you're doing it again.'

Julia had not heard. She eased one elbow by putting a hand under it, and then with a mutter of irritation removed the hand to push back some hair that was falling into her eyes.

'Julia,' said Amy loudly. 'Mamma said you weren't to kneel on the floor like that.'

Perhaps the soreness of her elbow or the tickling of the hair in her eyes made Julia conscious of the outside world, for she usually needed more rousing than this. She sat up with a start and ran her fingers through her hair.

'You're on the floor again,' said Amy rather smugly.

Julia stared at the stripes on the tiger rug. 'I don't know how I got here,' she said unbelievingly.

'You slithered, I saw you.'

'Has Mamma come in?' said Julia guiltily.

'Not yet,' said Henry from the window. 'But she will soon, you'd better put that book away.'

Sighing, Julia scrambled up. Amy snatched the book and closed it so that there would be no temptation. Her self-righteous way of doing it exasperated Julia, apart from the irritation of having Miss Young's *The Dove in the Eagle's Nest* taken from her in mid-sentence —it was like somebody snatching a delicious morsel just as it was half-way to your mouth. She made a dart at Amy, who dodged.

'Don't shake me,' she said loudly. 'You got into trouble for that on Saturday. From Papa too.'

Julia looked at her in disgust. 'What a little prig you are.' But she made no attempt to recover the book. It was perfectly true, she was not supposed to read in the morning (though she tried to, every day), and that position, crouched on the floor, had always horrified her mother. Her father, in high indignation a few days before, had told her, indeed, that unless she could sit in a more ladylike way he would put an end to this infernal reading altogether.

It was not that she meant to defy her parents. She would just stretch out a hand for a book, only meaning to look inside and then put it down. But before she knew where she was there was somebody calling her angrily to come for a meal, and she would find that hours had passed. Reading in the Gresham household was a difficult matter, there were always so many other things that were supposed to be done, and books were regarded as a last resort for an invalid, for Sundays, or for a very wet day.

She went over to the window and peered out gloomily. Outside, a light drizzle was falling, and the two large dray-horses of the pantechnicon that stood outside the next door house had been covered up with bits of sacking. The pavement was strewn with straw, and as the children watched, a man from inside the van struggled to the tailboard with a packing case and heaved it on to the shoulders of his mate, who was standing in the road.

'Another box,' said Henry. 'That makes seventeen. What could be in them?'

Julia screwed up her eyes short-sightedly and pressed her nose to the window. 'I don't know. It looks as if they're covered up.'

'Of course they're covered up,' said Amy impatiently. 'Anybody who wasn't as blind as you are could see that.'

'I'm not,' Julia began. She never would believe that the grey blur she saw as the background to everything was not what everybody else saw. Besides, she was very touchy on the point; her parents frequently used her bad sight as a reason why she should not read so much—she looked so uncouth, they told her, hunching up her shoulders and peering at the pages. Captain Gresham would add that he was not going to have a girl of her age wearing spectacles, she was enough of a blue-stocking without that.

But Henry interrupted. 'I haven't seen any children yet,' he said mournfully. 'Only furniture men. I'm sure if there were going to be any children I'd have seen them by now.'

Amy came back and elbowed her brother and sister out of the way. 'It'll just be more old ladies,' she announced. 'And they'll be even worse about us being quiet and about complaining to Papa if we aren't.'

'And they'll have dogs—yappy ones,' said Henry, thinking bitterly of the pug a few doors up who barked until its eyes nearly fell out, every time he passed it in its front garden. And it made him particularly resentful that its owner had more than once accused him of 'setting the dog on'.

Henry had once said that Clifton road was inhabited by Greshams, by old ladies, and dogs. He was the one who felt it most. Julia was two years older, and would have read all day long if she had been given the chance. Amy, too, found it easy to amuse herself. She was perfectly happy with her doll's house which seemed apparently to need spring-cleaning nearly every week, and constant changing of curtains and bedclothes. Amy looked upon it as a duty and took the responsibility very seriously. But Henry was always restless; Clifton road was cramping, there was no one to play with, and the garden was far too small.

Indeed all the gardens in Clifton road were small. Melsham was an area of south-east London that had been very fashionable in the 1860's. The roads were broad and full of trees, the houses large, and many had coach-houses and stables. But since then the tide of fashion had moved further out and by 1891 the fashionable area where really prosperous people lived lay four or five miles beyond Melsham, or right in the middle of London.

The houses in Clifton road were large, but the people who had built them had not been able to afford coach-houses and stables and spacious gardens. Indeed, they had a miserable look of being built as close to each other as was possible without being positively joined on to the next house, and the gardens were pitifully small and pinched and surrounded with walls and high hedges that shut out most of the light. The Greshams, who lived at number 22, disliked their own garden intensely. It was cramped and ugly, and there were only two trees in it, a puny apple tree that bore hard apples every second year only, and was too small to climb, and a curious shrub with large shiny green leaves that their father called a castor oil tree.

But next door, in number 24, there was a magnificent

apple tree that reared itself up above the huge privet
hedge separating the two gardens. Henry had always
yearned after it. He had not much experience of climbing trees—the opportunity did not often come—but he
was sure he could manage this one, and he used to
lie on the worn grass in his own garden and stare up at
the branches and work out the footholds. Number 24
had other advantages too. There was a large conservatory attached to the wall of the house; it had a vine
inside and a certain amount of coloured glass in the
upper part of the panes. By hanging out of the boxroom window Henry could make out wooden staging
inside where potted plants had once stood. He thought
vaguely that it might do as a theatre if only he could
find somebody like-minded to play with.

But he had never been inside number 24. For as long
as he remembered, the house had been occupied by two
old ladies, so old and so frail that they never set foot
outside except on Sundays, when a four-wheeler cab
called, took them to church, and brought them back
again. Julia had a faint memory of being taken there by
her mother, and being given an album of watercolour
paintings to look at while the grownups talked. But
that was a very long time ago, and since then the
old ladies had altogether given up visitors. Then, in June,
the older and the frailer of the two had died, and
her sister had gone to live in Bournemouth with a
married niece. (The Greshams would not even have
known this if the deaf, elderly maid of the old ladies,
after years of holding herself aloof, had not thrown
off her reserve on the day of the funeral, and spoken to
Ellen, the house-parlourmaid at number 22, who had
passed it on to the children.)

A 'For Sale' notice appeared outside the next door
house, and for many weeks it remained empty, its
windows becoming darker and darker with dust, and

two or three panes of the conservatory broken by the stones thrown by passing boys. The grass in the garden grew high like hay, and the Gresham children hoped that the house might stay empty till the autumn so that they would have the benefit of the apples that fell from the tree on to their side of the hedge, instead of having to take them round to the owners of number 24.

But when they came back from their summer holidays they saw at once that the 'For Sale' notice had gone, and since then Amy had spent most of her time watching the house. She and Ellen supplied the household with news of all the comings and goings in the road; Julia was too short-sighted to notice much, and besides, was usually reading, and Henry was shy and self-conscious, which was no use at all if you were going to pick up bits of gossip from tradesmen and errand boys.

Then Amy had announced that windows in the next door house were open and that she had distinctly heard the sound of footsteps inside. Yesterday she said that the milkman had told Ellen that milk deliveries were to start the next day, and ever since early this morning she had been standing at the dining-room window watching the new arrivals. Henry had joined her. There was nothing to do, and he always felt particularly dispirited at this point in the holidays. It was not that he liked the three weeks spent at the sea; he hated having to bathe and being told continually that he was enjoying himself. But there was an organized daily routine at the sea, of going down on to the sands and plodding back to their rooms for meals. Once back home there was nothing, and the delight of being released from school had long since worn off. He stared out at the pantechnicon.

'Another packing case, that's nineteen. They must have got ornaments and things inside. It probably means more old ladies.'

'Even if there were children they mightn't be our age,' Julia pointed out.

'Or Suitable,' Henry said gloomily. The Gresham children had had many difficulties with their parents over this point. It had been decided that Julia could not go to the High School because the girls there were not always Suitable, and Henry had more than once tried to invite Unsuitable friends to tea. It hit both of them hard, because Julia did not like Holly Bank School, and longed for the High School, and as for Henry, he was the loneliest of the three of them and longed for friends.

At this moment Amy started calling to them from the other side of the house. They didn't answer at first, and her voice rose to an impatient shout.

'You'd better go,' said Henry. 'Last time we didn't she'd got her head stuck between the bars in your bedroom.'

They found Amy in the room that she shared with Julia. Her head was not stuck between the bars, however; she was standing on a cane-bottomed chair peering over the top of them.

'There is a boy,' she announced. 'I can see his knees in that room with french windows.' (The next-door house was in the shape of an L, and the part containing the french windows stuck out a long way into the garden, facing the fence and the privet hedge that divided the two gardens.)

'How do you know it's a boy?' Henry dragged over the other cane chair.

'Nobody else would show their knees, would they?' retorted Amy. 'Anyway, I've seen a girl too. She was throwing a ball against that wall until she saw me. Then she put her tongue out and went away.'

'She put her tongue out?' Julia was aghast. It certainly did not sound as though their parents would consider these children Suitable. 'Are you sure? How old was she? Anyway, it's raining, she can't have been playing outside.'

'Well, she was playing, and she did put her tongue out. And I put my tongue out too *and* my fingers to my nose,' said Amy with deep satisfaction. 'She's gone down by the conservatory, I expect she's in the front garden. I'm going to look.'

'You'd better see whether Mamma's come in first,' called Henry as Amy ran down the stairs.

Amy did not bother. She flung open the front door and ran out into the rain, and the others following her saw her peering through the privet that divided the front gardens.

'Come in, Amy,' Julia called. 'You'll get soaked, and you know we aren't allowed in the front garden.'

'She's there,' said Amy, returning. 'By the gate, watching the men. Shall I go and talk to her?'

'Go and ask her what her name is,' Henry said, never expecting that she would.

'All right, only I'll say that you sent me.'

Before they could stop her, Amy had darted out of the gate and had disappeared. Still standing in the front door, Henry clutched at Julia and giggled. 'She's going to do it.'

'Of course she's going to. You shouldn't have said that if you didn't want her to.'

They both listened. There was a sound of heavy boots walking over uncarpeted floors from the next house, and echoing voices that suggested empty rooms. But no sound of Amy.

'She must be staring at her,' said Henry with alarm. 'You know how she does.'

'Well,' said a girl's voice from beyond the hedge. 'Do you think you'll know me again? But look a bit longer if you like.'

'Hullo,' they heard Amy saying cheerfully. 'What's your name?'

'Catherine Mary Jocelyn Holt, if you must know.'

'Oh, it isn't me that wants to know. It's them.' (Henry clutched Julia's arm in an agony of embarrassment.) 'Do you want to see them? I'll go and fetch them.'

In his nervousness Henry would have run inside, but Amy was too quick for him. She appeared at the gate. 'Her name's Catherine Mary something, and she wants to see you.'

Smiling stiffly and uneasily Henry walked out into the road. Ellen appeared in the front door, her hands cased in cotton gloves all black from cleaning the silver. 'I *thought* this door was open from the draught as was running through the house. Whatever are you about, Miss Julia? You know how your ma carries on about this door. And where's Miss Amy? Don't you go letting her play in the road, now, or your pa'll have the skin off you.' She shut the door with a bang behind them.

Amy's girl was standing on the bottom rung of the gate, sucking a stick of toffee. She did not look as though she particularly wanted to see Julia and Henry. In fact, she seemed rather sulky. She had straight black untidy hair and heavy black eyebrows, and a navy blue sailor top to her blue serge skirt. There was a long silence during which they all looked at each other.

'My name's Julia Louise Gresham,' said Julia at last, feeling that something must be said, however trite. 'It's Louise because of Great-Aunt Louise and Julia because of my grandmother,' she chattered on nervously. 'And this is Henry and the little one is Amy.'

'Little yourself,' said Amy with disgust. 'The old lady six houses up said I was very big for my age. She thought I was nine.'

At this moment Ellen threw up a bedroom window and shouted at them. 'Whatever are you a-thinking of, standing out in the road like that? And in the rain too. You just wait till your ma sees you, she'll be coming any minute now, half-past twelve she said, and that means sharp to the minute with her.'

'Oh, yes, we'll have to go,' said Henry, looking nervously up and down the road.

'What's wrong with the road?' said the girl indifferently, pulling the toffee away from her teeth so that it stretched out in a long glassy streak with a curl at the end. She looked at it in a considering way and then put it back in her mouth.

Julia looked at her hopelessly. She was very much afraid the girl was going to be dreadfully unsuitable in her parents' eyes. Swinging on the gate, eating in the road, sweets between meals—she felt full of foreboding. 'They don't like us being out here. I expect it's the old ladies, partly. There are masses of them in the road and they rap on their windows if they see us doing something that they don't like.'

'Like making faces at their dogs,' said Amy cheerfully.

'Are you allowed to eat in the road? We aren't.'

The girl took the toffee out of her mouth. 'Why ever should anybody mind? Nobody in this house would. Aunt B gave me sixpence to stay out of everybody's way, as a matter of fact. But if you aren't allowed to go in the road you'd better come in. You can't go into the house, though. What do you do if you go for walks? You have to go in the road then. Or aren't you allowed to go for walks either?' She had to get off the gate at this point, because two of the removal men came out of the house.

'You'd better get off that gate, young missy,' one of them called to her. 'Or you'll have your dad after you. And best take your little friends with you. We've got some 12-foot bookcases to shift and we don't want to break anybody's neck with them.'

'That's what happens if you stand in the road,' said Amy sagely. 'People tell you off.'

The girl did not seem to care. 'You seem to spend your life being told off. There's a sort of glasshouse round here, you'd better come in that.' She led the way round the house, over a dank mossy path to the conservatory that Henry had so often admired. 'Of course it may be locked,' she said, rattling the door handle. 'Or perhaps it's just stuck at the top. She threw herself against it. The first two or three times the door resisted, but at last the swollen wood yielded, the door burst open, and she stumbled in. There was a close stuffy smell inside. The Greshams followed her and Amy shut the door. The girl scrambled up to the top tier of the wooden slats. Some earthenware pots still stood there, festooned with cobwebs and holding the remains of long-dead plants.

'Who is that Aunt B that you talked about?' enquired Amy, looking her up and down with interest.

'She looks after us.'

'But why doesn't your mother?'

'Because she's dead, of course, that's why,' said the girl fiercely.

Julia and Henry felt very uncomfortable. It was the most unforgivable thing, to force a person to give information like that. You might guess, and fish delicately around, but ask outright, never. Now that Julia saw the girl properly she realized that something was wrong. She looked neglected. Her unbrushed hair was wrenched back with a greasy and frayed black ribbon, the blue serge of her skirt and blouse was crumpled and spotty, and there was a hole in her stocking.

'You've got a brother, haven't you?' said Julia hastily. 'Amy said she saw him through the window.' Too late she realized that this was not a very fortunate remark; it made it seem as though Amy had been spying.

'That's Richard,' said the girl, 'He's reading, he always is.'

'Not now he isn't, Woggle, not now.'

They all jumped and turned hastily. The door that led into the conservatory from the house had opened, and a very tall spindly boy stood there, smiling at them in what Julia thought was rather a patronizing way.

'Are these your friends, Woggle? You haven't lost much time.'

The girl took the toffee out of her mouth. Her face brightened and she looked eager. 'Richard, are you going to come and play? Do stop reading and come. These are the children from next door. I've forgotten what they said their names were—except the girl's called after a great-grandmother, or something.'

Julia and Henry felt rather slighted by the way she talked about them, but not Amy. She looked accusingly at the girl. 'You said your name was Catherine Mary something, but *he* called you Woggle.'

The spindly boy wagged a finger at her. 'She said her name was Catherine Mary Jocelyn Holt? Naughty, naughty Woggle, she knows that nobody calls her that.' He came over and tugged at her ear.

'*You're* not to call me Woggle,' she flashed out at the Greshams. 'You can call me Kate if you like. Richard, what are we going to play? You invent something.'

Richard put his hands in his knickerbocker pockets and swayed backwards and forwards. 'What an insatiable little creature you are, always wanting to play. But I don't know if I can, Woggle mine. Our worthy father wants me to help him put away his books. There is, besides, Aunt B to be reckoned with. She has some foolish notion that we are hungry and she wants to administer meat pies. Listen, I can hear her calling now.'

Through the door that led into the house they could all hear somebody calling a long way off. But neither Richard nor Kate made any attempt to move. The voice came nearer, and at last angry feet strode over the bare boards of the room beyond the door. A stout woman dressed in a very vivid shade of blue, with a feather boa twisted round her neck, appeared in the doorway. She had very red cheeks that Julia at once thought must be rouged, and a fringe.

'Why bless me, you were here all the time. Why couldn't you answer, I'd like to know, with me screeching at you till I'm nearly hoarse.' She patted her chest, which was heaving alarmingly under the feather boa. 'Look, there's meat pies for your dinners. I've put them on a piece of newspaper in that room where you've been reading, Richie. And you've found some little friends to play with already, well, if that isn't nice. No need for you to be lonesome, Kay, while Richie's at his reading.' She smiled at them in a jolly way; she did not look the sort of person to be cross for long. 'You'll have to come along to tea as soon as we've got straight.'

'We'd better go now, I think,' said Julia hastily, embarrassed by this talk of dinner, and feeling that if they stayed any longer it might look as if they were expecting to share the meat pies.

'Ta ta for now, then,' said Aunt B cheerfully. 'Come and look us up again soon.'

The Greshams ran to the gate. The removal men were sitting on the front doorstep now, unwrapping greasy bundles of paper and uncorking bottles. Just as they were about to push their way through their own gate Julia stopped the other two. 'Don't you tell Mamma anything about those children. Just say that we've seen them if you must, but nothing else—promise.'

'Did you hear that lady say she'd put the meat pies on a piece of *newspaper*?' said Amy, deeply interested. 'I thought it was only in books about the slums that people ate off newspapers.'

'Never mind, don't you go chattering about it to anybody. Not a single person, now mind.'

CHAPTER 2

Shall we go in?

The children could not hope that Mrs Gresham had failed to notice the arrival of new people next door; the pantechnicon outside, the street littered with straw and sodden bits of paper, the shouting of the removal men to each other, made it glaringly obvious to anybody, even if they did not set foot outside the house.

'I only hope the mess is all cleared up before Papa comes home,' said Mrs Gresham at the children's dinner. 'Disorder does upset him so much, and I don't want him to have to complain to the new people the moment they arrive.' She frowned anxiously. Much of her life was given up to worrying in case the Captain should be annoyed, and to keeping watch for things that might upset him. It gave her a tense expression and made her very strict with the children. 'I shall give them a few days to settle and then I will leave our card.'

'Who will you leave the card on?' Amy was interested.
'Their mother is dead.'

Julia became nervous. Amy had given it all away. Their mother must know now that there were children next door, and that they had already made contact with them; she braced herself to be questioned. But Mrs Gresham seemed to pass over this in the relief of discovering that there was no lady of the house to call upon. 'A widower. That does make things easier. Widowers generally lead very quiet lives. Papa will be glad of that, I'm sure.'

'I knew you'd do that, Amy,' Julia said afterwards.
Amy was aggrieved. 'Do what?'
'Go chattering about the children next door when I

particularly asked you not to. It only puts Mamma in a fret.'

'She isn't in a fret. And I didn't chatter, I only said . . .'

'Never mind,' said Julia hastily, anxious to avoid one of Amy's endless arguments. 'It's no good expecting anybody of your age to have tact. But don't you see, they'll stop us knowing those children.'

'It'll be all right when Mamma has called.'

'No it won't. As soon as she or Papa sees them she'll say they're unsuitable.'

So far the question of suitable friends had hardly touched Amy. She recognized that her mother discouraged her talking to the tradesmen and errand boys and other people's maids, but she had not much imagination, and accepted this as a tiresome adult ruling not to be taken very seriously. She had not suffered as Julia and Henry had, from not being allowed to make friends as they pleased.

It took a more mature female mind to appreciate all the things that grownups were going to disapprove of in the Holts. Certainly these did not at first occur to Henry. 'I don't know, Ju,' he said doubtfully. 'We've only seen them for about five minutes. Why isn't Mamma going to like them?'

Julia stared at him despairingly. She could not explain, it was a matter of subtle impressions that made it quite obvious to her that their parents were going to ban the Holts. 'They're so different,' she said at last. 'They haven't got a mother, I should think they do pretty well what they like. And their aunt has got a fringe and I should think she wears rouge.'

'Is *that* why her cheeks are so red?' burst in Amy. 'They *were* red, weren't they. I've never seen anything so red.'

Julia ignored her. 'If Mamma doesn't see them and doesn't call on the house then perhaps we can sort of

meet them by accident and play in their garden sometimes. So we mustn't go chattering about them and
make her think of them. Do you understand, Amy?' she
said sternly. 'And whatever you do don't say anything
to Papa.'

'But Mamma always does call on new people,' Henry
said mournfully. He had inherited his mother's worrying
nature.

'As there isn't a Mrs Holt perhaps she won't.'

'I do hope they won't stop us. That conservatory
looked wonderful. And there's the apple tree—we
haven't seen it yet. And that shed, it's three times the
size of ours, with a chimney too. Did you like the
children, Ju?'

'I don't know yet,' Julia said airily. But she was
certain that Richard, at any rate, was somebody after
her heart, though she could hardly dare hope that he
would be interested in her. He was so clever, he talked
in that marvellously grownup way, and he read. It
would be heartbreaking if their parents banned the
Holts as soon as they arrived.

For the next few days Julia and Henry were in a state
of high tension, watching their parents for signs that
they had made contact with the Holts, watching Amy
in case she chattered about them, and watching the
house next door for Richard and Kate. The removal
men had long since departed, leaving a litter of straw
and paper in the gutter which nobody had bothered to
clear up. But as it rained most of that week, Captain
Gresham did not seem to notice as he hurried past with
his umbrella up on his way to and from the train that
took him to his work in the City.

'There are new arrivals next door, Frank,' Mrs
Gresham observed at breakfast a day or two after the
Holts had moved in.

'That's who it is, is it,' said the Captain, raising his

head from the *Morning Post*. 'Saw a chap with carpet slippers shuffling out to the shed as I was doing my exercises this morning. Looked a bit seedy to me.'

'I understand he is a widower.'

'I hope he puts a bit of paint on the house, that's all. The Miss Brutons let things slide, and the place looks neglected; it spoils the road. And by the way, our own back garden is a disgrace. What is the use of my employing a man to keep it tidy if you children toss all your rubbish there the moment my back is turned. You don't deserve to have a garden. It's all got to be cleared up, mind, the instant it stops raining.'

It rained all that day, but next morning Mrs Gresham chivvied the children into the garden and told them to be sure the mess was all cleared up, otherwise they could have no pudding for dinner. The tin pails and spades that had been left on the grass were already beginning to turn rusty. Henry kicked a gaudy and dinted pail underneath the privet hedge.

'Thank goodness that's over for another year,' he said vindictively.

'You're glad the holidays are over?' said Amy, wide-eyed. 'I thought everybody looked forward to holidays.'

'Not me—bathing and learning to swim, with Papa holding up my chin and shouting at me. I'd rather stay here all my life than have a single day's summer holiday. Papa's there all the time, watching everything we do.' He peered moodily through the hedge.

'Can you see anything?' Amy asked.

'I can see their shed and the door into their backyard.'

'I mean *them*,' said Amy, stooping to pick up a red ball. 'Oh well, I expect they're like Julia, always reading. I'm going in to play with my dolls.' She was rather morose this morning.

'You can't. You've got to clear up the garden.'

'I've cleared up all *my* things a long time ago,' said

Amy haughtily. 'All the rest is yours. Look.' She kicked
at a ball with a hole in it, part of a wooden box, and a
bat. 'I say, won't Papa be waxy about you leaving out
your bat! Julia,' she called to her sister, who was leaning against the bars of the bedroom window with a
duster in her hand (she was supposed to be dusting the
ornaments on her mantelpiece, which was a job she
always shirked for as long as she could). 'Julia, Henry's
gone and left his bat out in the rain. Just won't Papa
blow him up!'

Henry took no notice. 'Ju, come down,' he called.
Julia disappeared. A moment or so later she came into
the garden, a checked duster still trailing from her hand.
'Shall we go in and ask to see those children?' Henry
said in a lowered voice.

'All right, why don't you. Is that all you called me
down for?' Julia began to wander in again.

'I mean, their aunt did say she hoped we'd come
again. And they've got that apple tree and conservatory
and shed, it's a jolly good place to play in. And I should
think that girl's lonely,' said Henry pleadingly.

'Go on, then,' said Julia. 'I'm not stopping you.'

'But you must come with me,' he said indignantly.

'I can't. I've got to finish the dusting.' Julia edged
away. It was one thing if they happened to meet Richard
and Kate by accident, and got invited into their garden,
but a completely different matter to ring the front door
bell and call on them formally. How did they know the
Holts wanted to see them?

'But I can't,' wailed Henry. 'What should I say I've
come for? Oh Ju, you must.'

Julia suddenly snatched the ball Amy was holding and
hurled it over the hedge. 'There you are. Now you've
got a reason for going in.' She ran back into the house,
jumped the three stone steps into the passage where the
coats were hung, and slammed the door with such force

that the coloured glass panes in it rattled alarmingly.

Amy gave a howl of rage. 'That was my best ball.'

'Tell Henry to go in for it then.' Julia's voice sounded muffled and far off.

'Go on, get it,' yelled Amy, hammering at Henry with her fists.

If there was one thing that alarmed Henry more than most it was ringing at strange doors, because he never knew what to say when people opened them. But he had hardened himself to asking for balls. The trouble on this occcasion was not that the people were strangers, but that he now did know them slightly and would be expected to talk.

'You'll have to do the talking then,' he said to Amy.

'No I won't. I didn't throw it. You always make me talk.'

Hoping that Amy would come round to it by the time she found herself on the Holts' front doorstep, but afraid to resist her in case she launched herself into one of her tantrums, Henry walked draggingly round to number 24. He pressed the bell and waited; Amy stood scowling beside him. There was silence in the house, nobody came. Henry's spirits began to rise, perhaps they were all out.

'That bell doesn't work,' said Amy accusingly. 'Go on, knock.' Then, as Henry hesitated, she seized the knocker and hammered thunderously. Somewhere in the depths of the house a door opened and footsteps pattered towards them. The door opened an inch or two and a very young and bedraggled-looking maid peered out. Her cap was on crooked, she had a large smear of dirt on her face, and the hand that they could see was covered with blacklead.

'Well,' she said, 'And what do you want? Just as I was blacking the master's grate too.' She gave a long, drawn-out sniff. More footsteps came up behind her.

'Maud,' said somebody, 'when will you learn to answer that door properly? That's no way to carry on. Who is it?'

Maud turned her head. 'Children,' she said. 'Don't know what they want.' She sniffed again.

The door was flung open and Aunt B appeared. She had a hat with a large red feather in it, a shiny red and black checked blouse with its sleeves rolled up and a black apron wrapped round her. She looked rather cross, but when she saw who it was her face lightened.

'Why, you've come to see the kids. (You be off back to your grate, Maud, or the master'll want to come into the study and it won't be ready.) Well, if this isn't nice. But they're still at their breakfast; we keep late hours in this house. Not like you, I'll be bound. I saw your pa setting off bright and early this morning. Come along in.'

She shut the front door behind them; there was no escape. Amy and Henry followed her through the dark hall, which smelt unaired and full of stale cooking. She ushered them into a room which apparently was a dining-room though it was stacked high with books. They stood in piles all round the walls, on most of the chairs, and on the mantelpiece. Round a table which had books and papers tumbled on to one end of it sat the Holt family at breakfast. It was an untidy-looking breakfast, the cloth only covered half the table and was stained with tea. There was an assortment of jam jars and cracked china with cups that did not match their saucers, and a huge brown enamel teapot. Kate was lolling back in her chair eating treacle with a spoon, Richard was holding a piece of bread and jam over a book and dropping jam on the pages as he read, while somebody, whom they took to be Mr Holt, was concealed behind a newspaper.

'Kay, just you stop eating treacle like that, you're spilling it all over the place, and that cloth's got to last

us the rest of the week. Queer to want that for break-fast,' she said in a conversational way to Henry. 'But there's no accounting for tastes. Give me plum jam any day. Well, I must be back to my bit of washing. Richie and Kay'll look after you.'

'Have some bread and jam,' said Richard. 'Where's your sister?'

'I think she's dusting,' said Henry desperately, wishing he was too, or doing anything but standing over these people's breakfast.

Richard wiped a blob of jam from the book. 'Your little sister looks very cross.'

'She is rather,' said Henry. As a rule he had not much to say, but embarrassment sometimes had the curious effect of making him very talkative. 'You see, they've taken away her cuddler today to wash it.'

'And what would her cuddler be?'

'It's a bit of towel that she takes to bed with her. But it gets a special sort of smell, and she hates having a clean one because it doesn't smell right and it takes a long time to get it right.' He looked at Amy for confirmation but she stayed obstinately silent. In an agony of nervousness Henry chattered on. 'It was worse about Dr Vonnister—that's her pink rabbit, you know.'

'*Mrs* Vonnister,' said Amy between clenched teeth.

'Oh yes, Mrs Vonnister. Dr Vonnister is her bear. She always takes Mrs Vonnister to bed too, but it got so dirty that Mamma told Mrs Marsh—that's the washerwoman who comes on Mondays—to put it in the wash. It dried the right colour, but all the stuffing seemed to have disappeared and it smelt terribly clean. Amy cried for a week after that.'

At this travesty of the truth Amy unsealed her lips. 'I didn't,' she said with great emphasis. 'It was only two nights.'

The newspaper rustled and Henry looked at it in a panic, being used to the irritable ways of fathers who disliked having breakfast interrupted by chatter. However, the face that was revealed over the top of the paper had a very mild expression, though it looked very clever, being thin and heavily lined. 'If you have finished breakfast perhaps you would like to run out in the garden and play.'

'Richard never does play,' said Kate disconsolately. But Mr Holt had lifted up the paper again and had forgotten about everything else. Kate sighed, scraped

back her chair and hurled herself at the door. 'Come
on,' she said to Henry. 'You can come and see Monarch.
I always groom him and Sultan after breakfast.'

Thankfully he followed her into the passage. 'Who's
Monarch?'

'He's my dog. He's an Irish wolfhound and very
intelligent. He's very noble too, I've got his pedigree and
it shows that his ancestors once belonged to kings.'

'Not a real dog,' said Richard, emerging from the
dining-room behind them. 'In case you are getting
alarmed. Just a figment of Woggle's imagination. Like-
wise Sultan, who is Woggle's purebred Arab stallion and
has his stables in the back room, side by side with my
books, I am sorry to say.'

Henry was thoroughly bewildered, but did not like to
say anything. He had never heard of children making
up things and talking about them seriously like this. It

G.G.   B

certainly would not be encouraged in the Gresham household.

Richard threw open the door of the untidiest room Henry had ever seen. There was a sofa, a few upright chairs and a battered armchair whose springs sagged right down to the floor, and all these were strewn with open books, torn pieces of paper, broken toys, old cardboard boxes, junk of every description.

'Woggle would not allow a single thing to be thrown away before we moved,' remarked Richard. 'We are paying dearly for it now. Still, as long as I can find my books I can endure it. Now, where is Monarch?' He tossed aside the debris on the sofa and finally produced a battered and dirty terrier dog whose straw was coming out of his paws. However, he wore a red velvet collar, which looked as though it was made by Kate herself, and a real leather lead.

'Monarch,' said Richard solemnly. 'Good dog, don't get excited. Woggle, you had better take him, he knows you better. Now, let me see, where is Sultan?' He knelt on the sofa and, rummaging behind it, finally dragged out a walking stick which had a stuffed sock fitted over the crook and some leather reins attached in rather a clumsy way. 'Woggle's milk white Arab steed who will allow no one else but Woggle to ride him. But he allows me to give him sugar. Here, boy, I've got some for you.' He fumbled in his pocket, produced something, and gravely held out his hand to the sock.

Amy was watching all this with a scandalized expression. At last she could bear it no longer. 'Why do you give that sock sugar? It isn't a real horse, it doesn't even look like one,' she said, scandalized.

'You'd better not tell that to Woggle,' said Richard calmly, 'or she'll threff you in the galophers till you quinkle.'

'There's no such word as quinkle,' said Amy in a loud

accusing voice. 'Nor galophers, either.'

'Isn't there, my little woman.' Richard sat down and lazily stretched out his hand for a book.

'Of course there is if Richard says so,' said Kate hotly. 'He gets it all from books. He reads all the time, terribly clever books that you couldn't possibly know about. King Arthur and encyclopaedias—everything.'

Amy grew red like a turkey-cock. 'There isn't any words like those that he said. There couldn't be.' She pressed her lips together in a way that Henry dreaded. He was more skilful than anybody at detecting the oncoming of one of Amy's tantrums and always did everything in his power to avert them.

'We really came in for a ball,' he said hastily.

'My ball,' said Amy accusingly. 'My best red one. Julia threw it over. On purpose, too.'

'Take them out and look for it,' Richard told Kate. 'And lose that child if you can.'

'Richard, *do* come out too,' Kate begged. 'It's so early, you can't want to start reading yet.'

'*We* aren't supposed to read in the mornings,' Amy said primly. 'Julia does, though.'

Richard lowered his book and looked at Amy in a dreamy way. 'What a jolly little person you are. You need taking in hand. Don't your brother and sister ever do anything about you?'

Amy, not really understanding this, decided to ignore it. 'I want my ball.'

'We'll all go and get it,' said Richard authoritatively. 'I can't have my poor Woggle bullied out of her senses by a little whipper-snapper like this.' He tugged at the french windows and flung them open. 'Now, just where did this famous ball alight?'

But Henry did not know. Usually he could tell to a foot or so where his balls fell when they went out of the garden, but he had not thrown this one, and was too confused to remember the direction Julia had hurled it. They all scattered round the garden, trampling down the tall untidy grass, parting clumps of plants, kicking aside the windfall apples that lay rotting on the ground. Richard found it at last. He held it up high out of Amy's reach.

'Here's a thing and a very pretty thing. What will you give me for this pretty thing?'

'It's mine,' howled Amy, hurling herself at him.

'I did not deny it. I merely asked what you would be willing to give in exchange for it. However, you had better have it in case you start crying.' He threw it down. 'Pick it up before Monarch takes it in his noble jaws.'

Henry giggled; this boy really did say very funny things. Kate started laughing too, and the more Amy scowled at her the harder she laughed. Richard merely raised his eyebrows as if surprised at this outbreak, and rocked himself gently backwards and forwards on his heels and toes.

'Come, come, Woggle,' he said at last. 'We can't stay here laughing all day, pleasant though it is. You told me to come and play. What do you want to play? I can give you sixty seconds in which to make up your mind.' He produced a heavy gunmetal watch from his waistcoat pocket and scrutinized it.

Kate licked her lips and looked around her in a frenzied way. There was a long pause. Henry stared longingly at the tree. If only he dared suggest that they might climb it! He was certain he could get right up to the top, the branches looked perfectly easy. He could hardly bear to stand still, he was trembling so with eagerness.

'Five seconds.' Richard said warningly.

Henry decided to be bold. His hands clammy with

nervousness, he had opened his mouth to ask when Kate spoke.

'Let's go into your house.' She was looking at Henry in rather a surly way, her black eyebrows meeting in a frowning line.

'No need to look so ferocious, dear Woggle,' said Richard, tapping her on the shoulder. 'I daresay your request will be granted.'

'Can we?' she said truculently to Henry.

This sudden turn in events had so startled Henry that he completely forgot about the tree. 'I suppose so,' he said weakly, not wanting it at all. 'There's nothing to do there, though.'

'We could just look,' said Kate, her face clearing a little.

So Henry led the way round to the back garden. At the top of the path that the tradesmen used past the side of the house and the back door, he stood back to let the Holts pass him. To his eyes the garden looked more dismal than ever. Huge lumps of white stone made an edge to borders in which nothing grew but ferns and withering goldenrod. The grass plot, too small to be called a lawn, was made even smaller by a flowerbed in the middle which was planted out with stunted geraniums. The Holts stared at it silently. Henry could think of nothing to say. Then Kate spoke.

'Can we go inside?' she asked.

Henry did not know what to say to this. You could not really refuse something that a visitor asked, but he trembled at the thought of what his mother was going to say. Julia had begged them to be so careful not to mention the Holts, and here he was, marching them into the house! However, Amy suddenly took the initiative.

'Come and see my doll's house. And the picture of Napoleon.' She took great pride in the immaculate neat-

ness of the doll's house (when Julia had owned it it had
always stayed in a wild state of disorder), and she loved
grownups to admire it and praise the way she looked
after it.

The schoolroom looked oppressively tidy and unused
after the tumble of the room that the Holts played in.
Ellen had just cleaned it and had departed, leaving the
window open a little at the bottom and a faint smell
of metal polish from the brass top of the huge fireguard. The table had been pushed back against the wall
and the green plush cloth arranged neatly over its
inky scars. (Julia and Henry always did their homework here, and dug at it savagely with their pens while
they searched for inspiration.) The ornaments on the
mantelpiece, the little weather house, the clockwork
drummer, the doll Aunt Ethel had brought from
Switzerland, the china bulldog, were arranged in a
straight tidy line, and the only sign that the room was
used for playing was the line of small dolls seated on
the window-sill; Amy had turned them out of the doll's
house while she was cleaning it.

The Holts stood and looked. 'So this is the doll's
house,' said Richard, 'Well, well.'

This was not what Amy wanted. They had not even
looked inside and seen how all the furniture had been
polished, and the new curtains she had just hemmed for
the drawing-room. 'Come and see Napoleon,' she said
aggressively.

They were on their way into the drawing-room to
inspect Napoleon when Julia came downstairs, roused
from reading uncomfortably on the floor by the sound
of strange voices. The duster still trailed from her hand.

'You've been reading,' said Amy accusingly. 'We're
just going to see the picture of Napoleon.' She threw
open the drawing-room door and ushered them in. Kate

lingered in the hall looking round her.

'Woggle likes what she sees, said Richard indulgently. 'Woggle secretly pines for an ordered life, don't you, Woggle?'

She hurried after them. 'It smells so *clean*. Where's the picture of Napoleon?'

There was no difficulty about seeing that. The picture nearly filled the whole of one wall of the room, above the table that was crowded with framed photographs of Captain Gresham in regimental groups. Napoleon stood on the deck of a ship, his arms folded, and a brooding faraway expression on his face. A group of English officers watched him (their names were written underneath the picture) with a sort of curious pity.

'I think it's the best picture in the world,' said Amy. 'And the next best is the tiger in the dining-room.'

Neither of the Holts seemed very much impressed. Richard stretched himself, Kate was gazing elsewhere in the room, at the highly polished brass on the mantelpiece, at the plants standing on the Kashmir shawl that was draped over the piano.

'Isn't it lovely,' she said suddenly. 'There's not a single book. Not one.'

Richard laughed. 'Poor little Woggle, hemmed in by an ocean of books in her own house. Well now, what about the second best picture in the world?'

So Amy led the way to the dining-room. The picture of the tiger was hung above the sideboard. It was a head, almost life-size, of a tiger with jaws opened as if it was about to devour its prey. It was the only picture in the room. Richard shuddered and turned to examine the other things on the walls. There were two framed documents announcing that the Queen had commissioned Captain Gresham and his father to be officers in the army; there were also some ancient pistols, two ceremonial swords and their scabbards, and quantities of daggers, which Amy said proudly were Afghan ones, captured by her father in India.

'You Greshams do seem to do a lot of killing.' Richard looked hastily at all the weapons round him. 'But fancy thinking about it while you eat.'

'All our family are soldiers,' said Amy furiously. 'Papa was a soldier until he had to go into the City, and Grandpapa was a soldier and his father too. And Henry's going to be one.'

'And you would be a field-marshal if only you weren't a little girl,' remarked Richard.

'No I wouldn't, I would be a clergyman because that's what the next eldest son does in our family. And Julia's going to be Great. At least she says she is, I saw it in her diary written out in capital letters. "I am determined to be GREAT" it said.'

Julia's face was bright red and she could hardly speak for confusion. 'I only wrote that when I was a little girl,' she mumbled.

'Anyway, she'll never be great,' remarked Amy coolly. 'She never does anything, she's always reading.'

'Whereas you will be great because you never read. But supposing Henry doesn't want to be a soldier?'

The Greshams looked at him in astonishment. None of them had ever thought that anybody could question this arrangement. They had accepted it since their earliest childhood.

'But that's what they always do, the eldest sons, I mean,' said Henry weakly.

So absorbed were they that none of them heard footsteps down the stairs, approaching the dining-room, till Mrs Gresham appeared round the door. She did not at first notice the Holts, who were standing behind it.

'Children, what is the meaning of this?' she demanded. 'Ellen has just cleaned this room and now here you are bringing in dirt from the garden and trampling it all over the carpets.'

Flushed with indignation, Amy rushed at her. 'Tell them that Henry's going to be a soldier,' she shouted. 'I keep on telling them, but they say what would happen if he didn't want to.'

CHAPTER 3

Two Tea Parties

No more unfortunate way of introducing the Holts could surely have been devised—the fact that they were in the dining-room where none of them had any business to be; mud from somebody's boots caked on the Brussels carpet; Richard and Kate looking decidedly unkempt (Richard had dribbles of egg-yolk on his waistcoat, and there were traces of treacle round Kate's chin), and Amy exploding with rage and just about to go off into one of her tantrums. But the surprising thing was the way in which their mother took it. Her manner suddenly became quite mild, and she said that they must be the children from next door, and she wondered whether perhaps they might be allowed to come to tea one day soon. (What the children could not know was that she saw this as an easy way out of the dilemma of whether or not to call formally on the Holts.)

'Oh yes please,' burst out Kate eagerly, and then, seemingly embarrassed by her eagerness, hung her head and shuffled with her boot.

'Very well then, I will write a little note to your mamma and ask her if you may.'

Julia and Henry were appalled at this gaffe of their mother's, and Mrs Gresham was aware of her mistake as soon as she had uttered it. Her cheekbones flushed a little and she said hurriedly : 'Perhaps your father is the right person to ask?'

Richard did not show a trace of embarrassment. 'Oh, Father doesn't bother about what we do, thank you.'

The upshot was that Mrs Gresham invited them to tea

on Friday afternoon, and said something rather weakly about leaving a card on Mr Holt before then.

Henry and Julia discussed it afterwards. 'I wish it had been the other way round,' Henry said longingly. 'Them asking us, I mean.'

Julia was amazed. 'But you hate going out to tea, you know you do. With strangers too.'

'But it looks so comfortable there, nobody seems to mind what you do. And their father doesn't look as if he ever gets cross with anyone. Mamma's so strict about manners and they mightn't have the right sort of ones when they come. I do like that girl, I wonder if she'd let me pretend about Sultan and Monarch too. Do you think Mamma will tell Papa that they're coming? He's the one that really stops us doing things. Oh Ju, do ask Mamma not to.'

'It isn't Papa,' remarked Amy, 'it's Mamma who stops us doing things because she's afraid of him being angry.' But neither of them paid any attention and Julia did ask her mother. At least, she could hardly tell her not to say anything to Captain Gresham, but she did ask whether her father knew there were two children next door.

'I don't know, Julia. So far he has only spoken about seeing Mr Holt in the garden in carpet slippers—which does seem a very odd state of affairs for anybody living in this road, after all Clifton road is in one of the *nicest* parts of Melsham. But if the poor man has no wife to look after him perhaps that explains it.'

'Does he know that they are coming to tea on Friday?'

'I don't think I have said anything about that yet. I shall probably mention it when the day comes.'

Julia had to be content with that, and she reported the conversation to Henry. 'Oh I do hope it's all right, their manners and everything. Mamma's bound to tell him if she doesn't like Richard and Kate,' Henry said dolefully. 'And then we'll get stopped from knowing them.'

At four o'clock punctually on Friday the Holts arrived. They came in through the front gate and rang the bell, and Ellen, in her black afternoon dress and frilly cap and apron, let them in and brought them to the drawing-room. They shook hands with Mrs Gresham, smiled faintly at the children, and then stood staring silently at the vase of ferns arranged in the empty grate.

They all had tea in the dining-room, in the shadow of the swords and daggers and the tiger which Richard had teased them about a day or two before. But Richard did not tease now, all his polished witticisms seemed to have left him, he might have been any other boy, and the word 'Woggle' never once passed his lips. He answered Mrs Gresham's questions politely and stared straight in front of him. It was perhaps disappointing that he did not show her how clever and amusing he was, but on the whole Julia and Henry were relieved that he behaved like the sort of boy they knew their parents approved of.

It was all very sober and quiet. Mrs Gresham sat behind the silver tray which bore the silver teapot and hot water jug. The second-best lace tea-cloth was on the table, which was laid with the same food that the Greshams always had when children came to tea— currant bread, damson jam, rock buns, sponge fingers, and cherry cake, all made by Mabel the cook general. The Holts took one piece from each plate in turn as it was offered to them, but they did not, as Amy noticed at once, eat their first piece of bread and butter without jam, as the Greshams had been brought up to do.

After tea Mrs Gresham went into the drawing-room, and the children into the schoolroom. The Holts still kept their party manners. They agreed politely but unenthusiastically when a game of ludo was proposed,

and when that had been played twice and Richard had won both times, the Happy Families pack was produced. At two minutes to six, Richard, having won every game (he seemed to know without effort who was holding all the cards he wanted), put down his hand on the table and said that they must go now. With a relief that was hardly polite the Greshams all jumped to their feet. Richard asked Julia to thank her mother, and with no further word opened the front door and, followed by Kate, walked down the garden path. The Greshams, standing there, heard first the gate of number 24 swing shut with a grinding of the hinges, and then, a few seconds later, in the distance, the garden door bang.

Henry sighed. 'Do you think they'll ask us back? It wasn't much fun was it? Do you think Mamma thought they were all right?'

'They didn't say "thank you very much for having me" to her,' said Amy. 'And they didn't have their first piece of bread and butter plain.'

'She might say it was because they hadn't got a mother.'

'She mightn't want us to know them if they haven't got a mother,' Amy pointed out.

Two days later Kate came to the front door. Ellen showed her into the schoolroom where Henry was playing draughts with himself.

'Can you come to tea tomorrow?' Kate demanded. 'Aunt B said we could ask you.'

Henry scrambled to his feet. 'I'll have to ask Mamma,' he said nervously, and pounded off in search of his mother, so frightened she would refuse that he could hardly speak when he reached her. But he came back jubilant.

'Mamma says we may, and to thank your aunt very much.'

It seemed very odd, when the time came, to walk down the road without coats and hats but wearing tea-party clothes, and just to turn into the gate of number 24. Rather nervously they stood on the doorstep (it was not very clean), and waited for somebody to answer the bell. Footsteps came pounding down the hall, and then slowed as they drew near the door. The door was pulled open a little way and Kate appeared.

'Hullo,' the Greshams said awkwardly. They stepped in and took a long time over wiping their feet. It was always difficult to know what to say when you arrived at other people's houses.

'Do they let you answer the door?' said Amy, who never suffered from shyness. 'They won't let us at home.'

Kate led the way down the hall. The house was very still, with closed doors everywhere. It seemed almost as if they had it to themselves. Richard appeared out of the back-room.

'You'd better come and see Aunt B.' He came up the hall and threw open a door. There, in a welter of pieces of material and half-finished garments draped over the chairs, sat Aunt B at a sewing machine. She removed a few pins from her mouth and smiled at the children and winked.

'How do you do,' they said.

'Excuse the mess. Hard at work as usual. A slave, that's me. My brother thinks he is, but between you and me . . .' She winked again. 'Ta ta, have a nice tea.'

'What's that room there?' said Amy, pointing to a door on the other side of the hall. Her curiosity was shameless.

'Father's study.' Kate threw open the door.

It was empty, though the feeling of Mr Holt's presence lingered in the room—the greyness of thousands of books stacked on the shelves (the sort of books that looked as though they had never been new), the smell of stale tobacco smoke and unopened windows, and the brown slippers in a grate that was littered with spent matches.

'All those books,' said Amy, gaping. 'And more in your dining-room. Whoever reads them?'

'Father, naturally,' said Richard, appearing behind her. 'That is why the room is called a study. S-T-U-D-Y— to investigate, acquire knowledge (as I do); in Father's case, to write books. Only at the moment he is reading still more books in the British Museum.'

'Where's your drawing-room then?' Amy demanded.

'We have no drawing-rooms here, drawing-rooms belong to polite society. There is a study, Aunt B's sewing room, Woggle's and my room (which we are proud to share with Sultan and Monarch), and the dining-room. That's all.'

'Well, you'd better not let Julia see all these books,' said Amy still staring at them. 'She'll just sit down and start to read.'

'An excellent idea. Would you care to?' Richard held the door back and looked politely at Julia.

'Richard, don't,' said Kate. 'It's bad enough with you, but if *she's* going to as well. Oh come on, let's have tea.' She dragged at his hand. 'Anyway,' she said to Julia, 'there are plenty of books in the back room, only have tea first.'

The back room was still as untidy as when they had first seen it, books and papers scattered round the end of the room that Richard seemed to occupy, and various battered dolls and their clothes at the other. The table, however, was pulled out into the middle and laid with a very lavish tea. Henry and Julia looked at it at once to count the places. (They always did this when they were out to tea, to calculate the number of grownups that they would have to deal with.) There were five plates and five knives—perhaps by some marvellous chance they were going to have tea by themsleves. Short-sightedly peering, Julia counted and recounted, hardly daring to believe such good fortune.

Kate was collecting chairs, tipping them forward to spill off the odd objects piled on them. 'Aunt B says do you mind drinking ginger pop, it'll save her making tea as it's Maud's half day.'

'Hands up those who spurn ginger pop,' commanded Richard. He scrutinized the Greshams, who put their hands firmly behind their backs and giggled, then he went to a sideboard where a collection of stone bottles stood. 'Sit wherever you fancy or wherever you can find a chair. And, look, I'd better explain the system. You don't wait for things to be passed to you. When you want something you say "I demand the cream horns" or whatever it is, and you go on demanding till you get them.'

It was a magnificent tea. Nothing there was home-made, all the cakes were the creamy, brightly iced ones that the Greshams saw in confectioners' but which their mother never bought; the sort of cakes she would call 'unwholesome'. Nor was there any cut bread and butter. There was a large loaf, so new that it squashed as you cut it, and a jar of strawberry jam; there were also crumpets and currant buns. Once they had tried it out, the Greshams far preferred the 'I demand' way. They were all of them naturally fast eaters, and usually suffered at other people's houses from trying not to outstrip everybody else. The relief of being able to eat at one's own pace was enormous, knowing that you would not have to sit hungrily staring at your plate until somebody noticed.

'I think we can say you Greshams have acquitted your-selves well,' remarked Richard towards the end of tea when the plates were beginning to look empty. He brushed some flakes of pastry off his waistcoat.

'Do you mean they've eaten a lot?' demanded Kate, looking tenderly at a piece of green marzipan on her plate; she had kept it as a last titbit.

'That among other things. They have also eaten fast and generally kept their end up. It was more than I expected of them, I must confess. Perhaps it was because they had no snarling tiger looking down at them.'

'That tiger picture's very valuable,' said Amy indignantly. 'Papa says so. He says it's a very good picture.'

'And what Papa says everybody must always agree with. Yes, yes, yes,' said Richard sadly, tilting back his chair. 'It's a pity; you're nice children on the whole.'

The Greshams looked at him, embarrassed and uneasy. They had never heard themselves discussed like this. Only Amy was truculent. She did not understand what Richard was talking about, but she suspected he was somehow making fun of them. 'What do you mean?'

'Woggle,' said Richard, 'you tell them. Do you accept what you're told, blindly and unquestioningly?'

Kate was nibbling at her marzipan and then holding it away and eyeing it. 'If you mean Aunt B, no, I don't and you know I don't. If you mean Father, well, he doesn't ever say much. There isn't anybody else, is there? Except the teachers at school and they're pretty silly, all of them.'

'There you are,' Richard told Henry and Julia. 'There speaks the independent mind of Woggle.'

'Do you mean we ought to disobey?' said Amy incredulously.

'Not at all. But you ought to try to develop an independent mind, all of you.'

'I don't know what that means,' said Amy flatly. 'But I don't want one, and I expect Henry doesn't because he doesn't like new things, and Julia doesn't because she wants to be great.'

It was only Richard who laughed. Henry and Julia
were too angry and embarrassed to see anything funny
about what Amy said, and Kate was bristling because
somebody was actually trying to disagree with her
brother. So Richard laughed alone, tilting back his chair
and laughing hoarsely in a way that the Greshams, eyeing him uneasily, thought was rather artificial.

'So Julia doesn't want an independent mind because
she's going to be great,' he said at last. 'If only there was
someone else to share the joke.'

Julia smiled uneasily, but she was still smarting horribly at Amy revealing all her most secret thoughts like
this. Kate could think of nothing else but the lack of
respect that was being shown to Richard. She glared
round at them all.

'Richard's the one who's going to be great,' she said
defiantly.

Amy was in one of her tough argumentative moods.
'How's he going to be great?'

'He's going to Christ's, then he's going to Oxford, then
he's going to be a professor and write books—books
that everybody will know about and read, even people
like you.'

Silence fell on all the Greshams at this. Even Amy was
quenched.

'To Christ's!' said Henry, awed. The Greshams had
never known anybody who was at Christ's. 'I thought
only dukes and people went there.'

'Richard's going to get a scholarship, of course.'

'A scholarship!' repeated Henry. He did not know
people who got scholarships either. There had once been
someone at Mr Edgar's school, where he went, who had
been considered clever enough to try for a scholarship
to Rugby, but it was before Henry's time, and anyway,
he didn't get it.

'Enough of this, Woggle,' Richard waved his hand. 'It

grows embarrassing. Besides, who is to say who will be great? It seems as though Julia here had dedicated herself to it from an early age, and young Henry will probably be our greatest and bloodthirstiest general, and Amy will be the lady who tells Prime Ministers what's what, threatening them with her umbrella as she does it. As for Woggle, she's determined to be a duchess. (Yes, Woggle, I've seen you dressing up to go to Court.) I tell you what, we'll form a society for the achieving of greatness, and I'll present the society's gold medal to whoever achieves greatness first.'

'You will,' interrupted Kate. 'When you go to Christ's.'

'Hush, Woggle,' said Richard reprovingly, 'don't be so partial. Let me see, what was I saying? Ah yes, greatness. Well, I think that before you can become great you will have to broaden your horizons a little, and enlarge your ideas beyond Clifton road and Papa. I'll take you in hand myself and see what I can do in the way of broadening and enlarging. The Society for the Achieving of Greatness, Broadening of Horizons, Enlarging of Ideas, and the Cultivating of Independent Minds we'll call it.' He screwed up his face and, taking out a pencil, started to scribble on the tablecloth. 'To simpify things we'll call it by its initials, SAGBOHEICIM, and that can be our password as well.'

'Will it be a *secret* society?' Amy had forgotten all her ill-humour in the fascination of belonging to a society.

'It can be as secret as you like. Let us put the matter to the vote, then. All those in favour of SAGBOHEICIM raise their hands.' They all shot up their arms, with such enthusiasm that they felt as though their shoulders would be dislocated. 'Those against?' Richard looked round enquiringly. 'Very well, the ayes have it, the Society for the Achieving of Greatness etcetera etcetera has been formed. Now the next thing we must do is to have an oath swearing eternal fealty to the society. (That means loyalty),' he added severely to Amy. 'Stand up all of you, and we'll drink a toast and swear an oath.'

'A toast like Papa's at Christmas dinner?' asked Amy, now deeply interested. 'The Queen, God bless her, and Absent Friends?'

'Of a similar nature,' said Richard.

'Are we going to drink it in gingerbeer? It's awfully difficult when there's only a little bit left at the bottom,' said Kate. 'Your tongue gets stuck in the bottle and you make such a funny noise.'

'You must just do the best you can to preserve decency. A future duchess ought to know how to manage.'

'Can we throw the bottles over our shoulders when we've finished?' Henry's face was flushed with excitement and his eyes were shining. 'They do it in some regiments, I don't know which.'

Richard looked round the room cautiously. 'If we do, we'll have to stand on this side of the table and throw the bottles back into the fireplace. We don't want to break the windows or the bookcase at the beginning of it all and get the society banned.'

So the five of them ranged themselves down one side of the table with their backs to the heavy black marble chimney-piece. Richard looked it up and down and then removed the clock that stood on it. 'Now,' he said, 'no laughing, this is a serious occasion, and I'm not starting until everybody has a straight face. Have you all?'

But everybody, with the exception of Amy, was struggling against laughter, and pursing their lips and screwing up their faces. Amy alone was deeply impressed with the solemnity of the occasion and was gazing at Richard, her bottle ready.

'The Society, eternal loyalty, the Society, may it prosper. SAGBOHEICIM!' pronounced Richard impressively.

'Woggle, you're laughing, we'll have to start again.' But it was too late, Amy had tipped back her bottle with a loud sucking noise, and had hurled it with a force that made her stagger. It crashed splendidly on the black marble and flew all over the fireplace, and everybody laughed and laughed until they fell on their knees, and finally rolled on the floor, clutching themselves and gasping and whooping.

CHAPTER 4

The Departure of Mrs Vonnister

The unfortunate thing was that Ellen rang the bell long before anything much had been decided about the Society. Aunt B let her in and showed her into the morning room, where she stood disapprovingly pursing her lips at the untidy state of the room, the dishevelled look of the children, and at the tea things, still on the table.

'But it can't be time to go,' said Henry. 'Why, we've only just had tea, it's only about a minute since we came.'

'I can't help that, Master Henry. Time it is and more. Now don't keep me waiting, there's a good boy, there's the table to be laid for you pa's dinner, and you know what he's like if it's a minute late.'

'What about SAGBOHEICIM, then?' said Julia in an undertone, lingering at the door.

'Tomorrow morning I'll deal with those. Now run home like good children,' said Richard benevolently.

This stung, and they were none of them in a good temper as they walked up the road and up the backpath that led to the kitchen door.

'I do think you might have left us a bit longer,' grumbled Henry. 'We were getting along so well too.'

'Six o'clock your ma said and six o'clock I came,' said Ellen. 'So don't you go complaining to me. Such a mess you've got yourselves into too, and I've never seen anything like the pigsty that that room was—somebody ought to be ashamed of themselves. And I can't think that your pa and ma are going to like you playing with those children, that aunt of theirs a dressmaker and all.'

Henry and Julia felt a rush of fear. So the grownups had decided already that the Holts were Unsuitable, and now they were going to be separated from them. They were in the kitchen by now, where Mabel was ironing shirts on the table. There was a hot singey smell, and folded shirts were draped over a clothes horse, airing in front of the fire.

'How do you know she's a dressmaker?' Julia asked indignantly.

'That's what that maid of theirs told Mabel, isn't it, Mabel?'

Mabel nodded and held up an iron to her cheek to see how hot it was. 'If you can call her a maid. Poor sort of little thing she is, hardly fit to be in service at all. Now out of my way, there's good children, I've got these shirts to finish. You'll find your milk and biscuits in the schoolroom.'

'I don't see what's wrong with being a dressmaker,' said Henry, taking angry bites out of a Marie biscuit.

'I'd rather do that than spend all my time paying calls, like Mamma and her friends do,' said Julia passionately.

'Ju, we must go on seeing them. It's the first children we've ever had in the road, and they're just the right age. There's so much we can do with them, too. The apple tree and the conservatory and the huge shed—we haven't even properly seen their garden yet.'

'And I want to belong to the secret society,' said Amy.

'They'll stop it if they hear about the dressmaking,' Julia said gloomily. 'There was that boy Peter Dawlish whose father was a dentist. They stopped that.'

'They just mustn't hear, that's all.' Henry thumped the table with his fist. 'And Amy, if you go gossiping and telling tales, there won't be any society for you to belong to.'

'Supposing Mabel or Ellen do?'

'They won't, I'll make them swear on Mabel's Bible.' Henry spoke with unusual determination. 'They won't after that. I'll go and do it now.' He jumped up from the table and went. Julia, listening to the slam of the door, felt that the Society and Richard had already braced up Henry and made him act with more authority.

Ellen and Mabel swore. They were not disobliging creatures, and as Henry pointed out, if he and Julia and Amy could go out and play next door, they would be less likely to get in the maids' way when they were cleaning. Besides, Mabel said she had an aunt who was a dressmaker and a more respectable body never walked this earth. No, as long as the children were good, Ellen and Mabel promised they wouldn't go making any mischief with their ma and pa, but if they were naughty, mind, and started being rude . . .

But next morning, when Henry lay huddled in his bed, listening to the sound of his father moving about the dressing-room next door and waiting for him to stride in with the Indian clubs, he had a sudden thought. Today was Saturday, and though he usually went to the City on Saturdays, today Captain Gresham was staying at home. It would be quite impossible to go into the Holts' house while their father was about. The Society would have to wait till Monday. But how would they tell Richard and Kate this?

Captain Gresham threw open the door and strode over to the window, swinging his clubs zestfully. Henry peered at him over the top of the bedclothes as he flung open the window at the bottom, letting in the chilly air of an early September morning.

'Fine day, a little damp, perhaps, but the rain will probably keep off. Don't dawdle, Henry, at your age you ought to be leaping out of bed.'

Henry hastily pushed off the bedclothes, shuddered

as his bare feet stepped from the small mat by the bed on to the cold oilcloth, and went and fetched his clubs from the cupboard. They went through the same exercises as they always did, but Henry, because he was thinking about the Holts, did not concentrate, and got left behind. Captain Gresham was impatient, and Henry, in his nervousness, overbalanced when they were doing the knees bend exercise, which irritated Captain Gresham still more.

'Lack of concentration, that's your trouble, Henry. You'll never get anywhere without it. Julia's as bad, always burying herself in a book, but it's not so bad for a girl. Pull yourself together. How are you getting on with those boxing exercises now?'

Henry hung his head and muttered something about not having had much time.

'Now if there's anything I hate it's prevarication and excuses about time,' said Captain Gresham fiercely. 'Anybody has time. It's just a question of wanting to do a thing enough. Now stand up and take that hangdog expression off your face. Slouching and muttering never made a soldier.'

There was no chance of telling Julia anything over breakfast, though Henry kept on trying to catch her eye with agonized contortions of his face. Captain Gresham was reading extracts from the *Morning Post* and commenting on them angrily to his wife, but he did at last notice Henry.

'What's the matter, Henry? You look as though you've swallowed a mouse.'

'I think he wants to tell Julia something,' Amy observed.

'If you want to say something, speak up like a man. I can't bear underhand, sneaking ways. What do you want to say?'

'Oh nothing, Papa, really.' Henry hastily took a gulp

of tea which washed a crumb down the wrong way, so that he nearly choked. For ten minutes after that he gasped and his eyes streamed and he was quite incapable of saying anything. Captain Gresham gave him irritated looks and went on telling Mrs Gresham how ridiculous he considered it to appoint Mr Gardner Minister of Agriculture. 'Knew him at school, hadn't the wits to get into Woolwich or Sandhurst, so he went into politics instead. That's the sort of man who governs our country nowadays, my dear.' He flung down the paper and pushed back his chair. This was the signal for the children. They muttered their grace and bolted for the schoolroom.

'What *were* you trying to say at breakfast?' Julia demanded.

'It's Richard and Kate. I just thought this morning when we woke up. We can't go in, not while Papa's here. We'll have to wait till Monday. How are we going to tell them? I mean, we can't go and say that we don't think Papa would like us to know them, can we?'

'Papa might like them,' said Amy. 'Though *I* don't much.'

'That's because they put you in your place,' Julia told her crossly. 'Which nobody else does.'

Amy took no notice. 'Still, I want to join that secret society. Why don't we go and ask Papa if we can play with them?' Amy was alone among the Greshams in not being afraid of the Captain. She was very much his favourite and occasionally, when Julia or Henry were hard-pressed, they used her to beg favours. But not today.

'Amy, you're not to ask Papa anything of the sort,' Julia said hotly. 'You don't want to be stopped from going in next door, do you? Well, just do as you're told then.'

'Papa would probably like them. That boy's going to Christ's.'

Amy said things that anybody else would be ashamed even to think of. Her brother and sister stared at her, outraged. '*Amy*, how *could* you?'

She was not at all put out. 'It isn't me that likes him because of that. I don't care what school he's going to, I think he's stuck-up and gives too many orders. I just said . . .'

But she was interrupted by a distant shout from the

other garden. 'Are you going to come in? Henry and Julia, are you going to come in?' A pause, then the voice became exasperated. 'Richard says, are—you—going—to—come—in?'

The Greshams all looked at each other. 'We'll have to go out.' Julia said urgently. 'Quickly, now, before Papa hears. Walk *quietly*.'

They tiptoed out of the room, drew down the bolt of the garden door as quietly as they could, and ran into the garden. At the top of the garden, where the wall at the end met the privet hedge at right angles, there was a gap where the privet did not grow. It was the only place in the garden where you could not be seen by people looking out from the house and into this gap they all squeezed themselves.

'Kate!' called Julia in a low voice. 'Kate, we're here.'

There was a swishing noise on the other side of the fence as Kate walked through the long grass. 'Where are you? What are you whispering for?'

Julia stood on her toes and peered over the top. 'Here, at the end. I don't think we can come in today. Would Monday be all right?'

'Not come in today? Why ever not? We got up specially early and made Maud give us breakfast before she'd even done the steps. And pretty cross about it she was too. And Richard's waiting for you, he's not even reading, for once.'

'Papa's calling us,' announced Amy, who was at the back.

'We'll have to go now,' Henry said fearfully, pulling at Julia.

'We'll come in on Monday then.' Julia did not wait for Kate's answer, but extricated herself from the gap and ran in, her face smudged with black from the privet.

They kept well away from the garden all Saturday

and Sunday, or, if they had to go in it, kept their voices very low so that Kate would not hear them and come out. But Julia wondered uneasily whether Kate had taken offence, and just what was going to be said on Monday.

The Gresham children always looked forward to Mondays. Sunday was a great strain, with their father with them all day, liable to question them about the sermon, about their lessons, or about what they had done during the past week. Until they climbed into bed on Sunday night they did not feel free from danger, and they always woke up on Monday quite light-hearted. When the door shut behind their father at quarter-past eight, and they knew they would not see him till half-past six that evening, Julia and Henry felt an enormous sense of freedom. It was as if the holidays were beginning all over again.

'We'll have to wait for an hour at least,' Julia said on Monday morning. 'You know how late they usually get up.'

'What are you going to do?' Amy asked. 'Go and knock at their door, or call them like Kate did us?'

Nobody had thought of this. 'I'm not going to go and knock at their front door,' Henry announced. 'It was bad enough the first time with that maid saying what did I want.'

'Henry, you'll have to,' Julia wailed. 'You know I can't by myself, a girl can't do anything like that. I'll come with you.'

Henry shook his head. When he was nervous he often became surly and silent, and this time he picked up a book of Julia's—it was a selection of Mrs Hermans's verse, and she knew he could not possibly want to read it—and not another word would they get out of him.

'I'll go to the front door,' said Amy.

'You can't. Not without Henry.'

'Well I want to have this secret society, and if you're not going to do anything about it then I'll have to by myself. It's all right, I'm not going to knock at any front door.' She rushed out of the schoolroom, and a minute or two later they heard her in the garden, chanting monotonously: 'Richard and Kate, are you going to come out?'

Henry was roused. 'You'll have to stop her doing that. You'll have the Old Dame complaining. (The Old Dame's house lay beyond the wall at the top of the garden; she was the most dreaded of all their elderly neighbours.)

'Here comes Kate,' called Amy with satisfaction (she was standing on an orange box and peering through the privet). 'Here I am, I can see you.'

'I don't care where you are,' Kate said crossly. 'You'd better keep quiet, Richard's working.'

'He can't be working. What at? It's still holidays.'

'He doesn't have school holidays,' said Kate disdainfully. 'He works for his scholarship all the time. Three days a week he goes to read Latin and Greek with Mr James, and the rest of the time he does it by himself, or with Father.'

Richard spoke from inside the house, he sounded weary. 'Don't argue through a hedge, Woggle, it's undignified. If you must argue, fetch that little girl in and do it somewhere quietly where I can't hear you.'

'I'll come in then,' said Amy jumping off her box. 'Only you'll have to wait until I've put this box away.' She stowed the box tidily in the shed (she had inherited her father's methodical habits). 'I'll get Henry and Julia,' she called. 'They want to come too.' She came over and rapped on the schoolroom window. 'Come on, Richard says we're to go in.'

Henry no longer pretended to read. 'Are we going to tell Mamma we're going in?'

'She's gone up to London, don't you remember?'

Henry jumped up with alacrity. 'Come on, then. We can just say to the maids that we're going next door.'

It was washing day. The scullery was a fog of steam from the clothes boiling in the copper, and Mrs Marsh the washerwoman, her face red and shiny, her sleeves rolled up well above her elbows, stood prodding at the seething and bubbling mass of white linen. The smell of boiling clothes filled the kitchen and the maids were not to be seen anywhere. So much the better, Julia thought.

'Will you please tell Ellen that we've gone into the next house for a bit and we'll be back in plenty of time for dinner, so she needn't call us,' she said hastily to Mrs Marsh. Mrs Marsh was a great talker, and you always had to say what you wanted as quickly as possible and then escape, otherwise she would keep you for hours.

'That's right. Young folk don't need much bidding where their dinner's concerned. All except my Eddie, he was a poor eater if ever there was one. Many's the time he said to me, "Mum," he said . . .'

But Julia never heard what Mrs Marsh's Eddie used to say; she had fled, and with Henry and Amy behind her, ran into the Holts' garden. They found Kate sitting morosely on the edge of a tea chest which had been tossed down by the shed door. Monarch was on the path beside her. She looked at them all coldly.

'Hullo, what do you all want? And who said you could come in here anyway?'

The Greshams stopped still, much discomfited. 'I thought Richard wanted us to come,' Julia faltered.

'Well he doesn't, nor do I. All he wanted was for that little sister of yours to stop shouting while he was working.'

'But he's going to do the society, he *promised*.' Amy was outraged.

'That was on Saturday. You wouldn't come then so you've lost your chance. Why should we go hanging round waiting for your beck and call?'

This was dreadful. You could not start quarrelling with people when you hardly knew them at all, and the sort of things that Kate was saying were only permissible to a brother or sister. Henry, who was a great lover of peace, became almost tearful in his efforts to put things right.

'We're terribly sorry, really we are. It was just that we forgot that the day you said was Saturday and that Papa was home and was going to take us out and things, so we couldn't come in, and then we heard him calling us so we had to go at once.'

'You seem to be terribly afraid of your father,' said Kate coldly.

'Yes, they are,' announced Amy. 'So's Mamma. I'm the only one that isn't. I don't mind what I ask him, but they're too frightened even to . . .'

Heaven knows what fearful things Amy might not have revealed to Kate at this point, but mercifully she was interrupted. The french windows were flung open and Richard appeared. He stood blinking at them all, like a pit pony that had suddenly been brought into the light. 'Woggle, I must ask you to keep these friends of yours quiet. How can I be expected to work when . . .'

But Kate flung herself on him and clutched him violently round the neck. 'Oh Richard, don't go on working, dear, good, kind Richard, just this once, come and play with us.'

'There's the society,' Amy pointed out accusingly. 'You said you were going to do it. Papa says a gentleman should always keep his word about everything.'

Richard looked at her moodily, his lower lip thrust

out. 'She prattles about a society—what society is she referring to, do you know?' he appealed to the others.

'It was the society for broadening our horizons and things,' Kate said eagerly. 'Do let's make the rules. I'll go and get a paper and pencil.'

'And can we have a secret code and secret signs and things?' Henry said excitedly. 'We could have a post office too, between the two houses.'

Richard held up a weary hand. 'Enough. If I said the society was to broaden horizons, then that is what I shall do. A gentleman keeps his word.' He bowed in Amy's direction. 'You will find me in the conservatory. Woggle, bring them along to me in two minutes' time.' He walked away down the path.

The others clustered excitedly round Kate. 'What's he going to do, do you know?'

Kate shook her head, she had started to count aloud. 'When I've got to a hundred and twenty we'll go. Now don't interrupt.'

They watched her, almost shivering with excitement at what lay ahead. Richard seemed to make everything that he did and said important.

'A hundred and nineteen, a hundred and twenty,' Amy finished with Kate. 'Come on, let's go.'

'I'm coming. Only I warn you, he's in his king mood. You'll have to kneel down and say "my liege lord, I crave audience" if you want him to speak.'

They hurried down the path by the conservatory, peering eagerly through the grimy panes. Richard was sitting there, on the top tier of the staging, clasping his knees and looking very remote. They burst in through the door and stood eagerly staring at him. But Richard took no notice at all. With a faraway expression on his face he stared up at the glass panes of the roof. They shuffled uneasily on the gritty floor, feeling that perhaps he could not have heard them come in. Then Kate remembered.

'My liege lord, we crave audience,' she said, bowing her head respectfully.

Then at last the huddled figure sitting above them seemed to become aware of their presence. Slowly he gazed down at them.

'Is the child known as Amy Gresham of your number?'

'Here I am,' Amy said eagerly, fascinated and completely forgetting all her complaints about Richard.

'Let Amy Gresham advance.'

Kate pushed her forward. 'Kneel, can't you,' she muttered violently, pressing at her shoulder. So Amy did kneel on the blistered white paint of the bottom tier of the staging, gazing fascinated at the lordly and aloof figure above.

Wearily Richard contemplated Amy, in her brown holland pinafore, kneeling below him. 'It has come to our notice,' he said in a remote and measured voice, 'that you, Amy Gresham, who wish to be a member of that ancient and honourable society known as SAGBOHEICIM, are guilty of certain childish practices that it behoves you long ago to have abandoned. Wherefore, before we can admit you to our society as an aspirant to greatness, we must broaden your horizons and enlarge your ideas. We therefore command you, as from this day, to take leave of those unseemly practices that we have heard you are guilty of—to wit, the cherishing of objects known as a cuddler and as Mrs Vonnister. In token whereof, you will bring them to us here and now, to dispose of as we think fit.'

There was a complete hush in the conservatory. The children stood staring at the figure on top of the tiers of wooden slats, almost forgetting that it was Richard. It was like hearing a king or a judge speak, Julia thought.

Even Amy was deeply impressed. She had no idea what he was talking about, except that Mrs Vonnister had been mentioned, but she was mesmerized by Richard's air of regal authority. Nobody moved. Richard spoke again.

'Why are our commands not obeyed? Fetch the objects we have named.'

Kate recovered herself. 'Go and get them,' she told Amy. 'What he's talking about—you must know what they are.'

Amy scrambled to her feet. 'You won't do anything before I get back, will you?' she said urgently. With a slam of the door she was gone.

They waited there in silence, hardly daring to move. Richard sat with his chin on his knees, an inscrutable expression on his face, as he stared up at the sky through the dirty panes of glass.

Amy did not take long. Red-faced and panting, she rushed back clutching a bit of towel in one hand and a battered dirty toy in the other. She laid them at Richard's feet and stood back, staring at him eagerly. Slowly he turned his head to look at them. He raised his eyebrows with disdainful disgust as he prodded them with his foot.

'Remove them from our presence and place them on the floor.'

Amy obeyed without a protest, even though the floor was gritty and dirty. From his high seat Richard surveyed them.

'They are an unpleasing sight. The time is indeed ripe for their destruction.'

He stared down at Mrs Vonnister and the cuddler. Mrs Vonnister was certainly shabby. She was the same colour as the dirty tiled floor. The wool of her coat had worn threadbare and the straw of her stuffing bulged out of each of her legs. There were pits left where her eyes should be, and only two patches, a little cleaner than the rest of her face, showed where her ears had once been.

'Bring some rope,' said Richard suddenly.

They all darted forward in a frenzy, pushing and struggling to get out of the door first, and ran wildly into the garden. Henry in his excitement would have cut down the clothes line if Kate had not whipped the lead off Monarch's collar. She rushed back into the conservatory.

'We've got something,' she shouted. 'It's Monarch's lead, but he won't mind.'

Richard's face showed no excitement or surprise. He refused the lead. 'Wrap the creature in its shroud,' he said.

They did not understand, but stared at him, puzzled. 'Wrap it in that obnoxious rag,' he said impatiently. 'And knot it tightly.' Henry seized Mrs Vonnister, knotted the cuddler round her, and then looked at Richard for more instructions. 'Now you may attach the rope,' Richard said. This was more difficult, but Henry eventually tied the ends of the cuddler through the loop of the lead. Then Richard stood up and advanced down the staging haughtily. He picked the shrouded Mrs Vonnister out of Henry's arms, and holding himself majestically upright, stalked out of the conservatory. The children thronged eagerly after him, and clustered at a respectful distance as he stood on the grass.

'Mrs Vonnister, prepare to meet thy doom,' said Richard in a loud voice. Then he whirled the lead round and round his head. Beside themselves with excitement and not realizing what they were doing, the children started screaming.

'She's going, she's going,' yelled Henry. As he said it, Richard let go of the end of the lead, and screaming louder than ever, jumping up and down in their excitement, the children watched Mrs Vonnister in her white shroud soaring upwards, getting smaller and smaller. Then the speck started coming down.

'Wouldn't it be funny if it went down that chimney,' shrieked Kate. 'Oh do go down, do go.'

Mrs Vonnister obeyed. Down like a plummet she fell, neatly into the chimney of the house beyond the wall.

'It's the Old Dame's chimney!' said Henry, and he started laughing so hard that he fell down on to the ground, where he lay groaning and heaving and clutching himself and giving little snorts of laughter. They all laughed, except Richard who stood looking on with his hands thrust into his pockets, rocking backwards and forwards with an expression of mild surprise on his face.

'She hasn't gone all the way down,' announced Amy at last. 'I can see the red lead of her trailing out down the chimney.'

'You can always go and pull her out when you want to take her to bed then,' said Henry, and this thought sent him into fresh paroxysms of laughter.

'Fancy Henry laughing so much,' said Amy with interest. 'He doesn't often, and he's usually so frightened of the Old Dame. Well, can I join the society now?' she asked Richard in a challenging way.

He considered this. 'I will give judgement in the conservatory,' he said at last. 'You may follow me there in sixty seconds.'

They all counted sixty aloud together, and then jostled down the narrow path and back in through the door. Richard was sitting in the same place, as motionless and as aloof as before.

'My liege lord, we crave audience,' they shouted, giggling a little this time.

Richard looked at them. 'What is it you seek?'

'Well, I want to know whether I can belong to your society,' said Amy. She had lost something of her awe now. 'After all, I did do what you said, didn't I?'

'We decree that you must remain on probation,' said Richard in a measured voice. 'For at least four weeks, until it is certain that you are worthy. But take heed, if it comes to our ears that there is aught repining after the departed ones, all your pleading to join our ranks will be of no avail.'

Amy stared at him uncomprehendingly. 'Do you mean I can't . . . ?'

Kate shook her shoulder. 'He says you can join if you don't go moaning about that old rabbit of yours. But you've got to wait for four weeks. Isn't that what you meant?' she appealed to Richard. He inclined his head. 'What about the rest of us then? Can we join?'

'You must prove yourselves worthy.'

'How?' demanded Kate.

'Each in his turn will be tested. Let us make a start with the eldest. Stand forth Julia Louise Gresham.'

Her heart thudding with nervousness, Julia stepped forward and went down on her knees on the staging as Amy had before her.

'You aspire to greatness,' said Richard consideringly. 'What steps shall we take to deal with that?' Julia knelt there with her head bowed, not daring to look at him. 'Are you prepared to make a grand gesture to prove your sincerity?'

'Oh yes,' Julia said eagerly.

'A really grand gesture?' He considered. 'Then we decree that you go to Westminster Abbey and there lay a wreath on Lord Byron's tomb.' Richard rose stiffly to his feet. 'The audience is concluded.'

'We can go and buy the wreath this afternoon if you like,' said Kate.

'That's right,' said Amy eagerly. 'Mamma's out and it's washing day and there's nobody to take us for a walk.'

CHAPTER 5

'Do let me be buried here'

With Amy and Kate so matter of fact, Julia could not do anything else but pretend to be completely in control of the situation. She held her head high and tried to look calm, though secretly she thought that they just did not realize how stupendous a task she had been set. To go to London alone! To find Westminster Abbey! To buy a wreath! Any one of these things presented difficulties so enormous that she felt herself breaking into perspiration at the thought of them.

'Let's buy the wreath this afternoon,' said Kate. 'There are some beautiful ones in that shop in Station road opposite the church. We can take Monarch, he needs some exercise.'

'How are you going to take him without a lead?' said Henry boldly, hoping that Kate would not mind him playing this game too. Having said it, he became frightened, and looked nervously at her, afraid that she would take offence.

'Oh that doesn't matter. He always follows me wherever I go. Though it's a pity about his lead being in that chimney. It was the one Richard gave me last Christmas.'

Henry gave a happy sigh. Kate had accepted him, he felt. Julia, on the other hand, was rather annoyed. She thought she had a right to expect Henry, who was the worrier of the family, to do a little worrying on her behalf. So she did her best to agitate him after dinner by making a great show of putting a knife into her money-box and extracting the money. (It was an understood thing among the Greshams that money, once in

the money-box, should stay there until an adult had
been consulted.) With much jingling of coins she
pulled out a half-crown, five sixpences, and sevenpence
ha'penny in coppers.

'That's half a crown for the wreath,' she said aloud,
'and the rest for the train fare to London.'

But it was Amy who showed the most interest. 'What
are you going to do if the wreath costs more than half a
crown?'

Julia took no notice. 'Go and get your hat if you want
to come.'

'I'll go and tell the maids that we're going to spend our
Saturday money,' Henry said eagerly. 'It's true; I've
still got mine left, anyway.'

Kate was swinging on the front gate of number 24
when they went out to find her; they could hear its
creak as they went down the road. She had not bothered
to tidy herself, she had no gloves and there was a
smudge of dirt across her forehead. They marched down
to the shops three abreast, with Amy trailing behind
looking into every window that they passed. They
talked enthusiastically of the sort of wreaths they would
choose for their own funerals, and where they wanted
to be buried. Julia said she wanted snowdrops and
white rosebuds, and tears came into her eyes as she
thought of it. She would like to be buried somewhere
historic, a cathedral if possible. Henry said it was
awful to think of dying, and he didn't really know
where he wanted to be buried. How did they know
that people were really dead when they put them
into coffins, anyway? Supposing they woke up when all
the earth had been shovelled on top of them? Kate
said she wanted a wreath of artificial violets, Aunt B
had some, and they were prettier than real flowers, especially if you sprinkled them with scent. Besides they
would last for ever; for ages anyway. They were talking

so much that they would have passed Bound's if Amy had not stopped them. It was a shop with a large glasshouse attached to it, full of potted palms and exotic ferns and delicate lilies, and the windows were decked with velvet hangings and large and beautiful wreaths.

'I like that one,' said Kate, pointing to a magnificent wreath of arum lilies tied with purple ribbon. 'It looks just right for a man who was a poet and a lord. Come on, let's go and buy it.'

There was no dignified way of retreat now, matters had gone too far, so, as unconcernedly as she could, Julia pushed her way through the glass doors into the shop. It had a black and white marble floor and smelt deliciously of flowers and of the warm damp air from the glasshouse. She looked warily round. To her relief she saw that Mr Bound was in the cash desk today. He was a very dignified man who always wore a frock coat and a carnation in his buttonhole, and she dreaded that he might ask awkward questions about why she was buying a wreath. So she walked up to the lady assistant who was furthest away from the cash desk.

'If you please, I want a wreath. How much is that one with lilies and purple ribbon?'

'Ten shillings that one is, miss, but I'm sorry to say it's bespoke already. I can do you a very similar one at eleven shillings.' She went over to the window to fetch it. Wide-eyed with consternation the Greshams started at each other. Amy looked rather smug.

'I asked you what would happen if it was more than half a crown.'

Julia stepped towards the window. 'Oh but I don't think . . .' she began nervously. But the shop assistant had already brought the wreath out of the window. It was larger than the other though there was no ribbon. The children all looked at Julia expectantly, waiting for her to speak.

'But we haven't got very much money,' she said at last, blushing painfully. (She was always conscious of the way blushes showed on her pale skin.) 'Have you got any wreaths for half a crown?'

The assistant raised her eyebrows in what seemed a very scornful way. 'Oh no,' she said primly. 'All *our* wreaths start at seven and six. Mr Bound,' she called, 'this young lady is enquiring about wreaths. We don't do any under seven and six, do we?'

It turned out as Julia had dreaded. Mr Bound put down his pen and came over. He bowed to Julia, and ran his eyes over the others, perhaps, Julia thought in a flustered way, looking for signs of mourning.

'May I venture to hope there is no family bereavement, Miss Gresham. (It *is* Miss Gresham, is it not? though it is a long time since I have had the pleasure of seeing you here.)' He rubbed his hands together and looked discreetly at the floor. At this, Henry took the others off to inspect the goldfish pool at the far end of the shop.

'Oh no,' mumbled Julia. 'It's just that we thought of putting a wreath on somebody's grave. It really doesn't matter, thank you.'

'A wreath.' Mr Bound smiled blandly. 'Perhaps that is, if I may say so, a little ambitious for young persons. Now how about a nice little bunch of flowers. Pansies, say, and forget-me-nots? Very appropriate and quite in keeping with the occasion.'

With his own hands he pulled out a bunch of pansies from a bowl on the counter; usually one of the lady assistants attended to that. Julia watched miserably, humiliated and disappointed. It would be impossible to refuse them now, but how mean the bunches looked when she did so badly want to make a grand gesture. Mr Bound wrapped them in tissue paper, as carefully as if they had been orchids.

'What have you got there?' said Kate loudly as soon as they were out of the shop. 'That paper isn't big enough to have a wreath, not nearly.'

'It's some pansies and some forget-me-nots,' Julia said defensively. 'I hadn't got enough money for a wreath.'

'If Richard said a wreath, then it'll have to be a wreath,' pronounced Kate. 'He's very strict about keeping to what he said.'

Henry, who could be very kind, squeezed Julia's arm. 'Couldn't you make a wreath yourself?'

In the end Julia did make it. She was exceedingly bad at doing anything with her hands, and she found this the hardest task she had ever attempted. She took an old hoop of Amy's (she didn't ask her, Amy would find a pressing use for it if she did). Such flowers as she had would nowhere near cover it, so she had to go out into the garden and surreptitiously snip at the golden rod. It was almost over now, its vivid yellow had turned brown, but it was the only flower the garden possessed, except the geraniums, and she did not dare take those. Captain Gresham inspected them every morning and knew to a bud how many flowers there were. Then she struggled with black cotton, trying to tie the flowers to the hoop. It was as difficult as trying to skip with a thin piece of string, it was too light and would not tie and kept tangling and losing itself; the pansies grew limper and limper as the afternoon passed, not only because of the cotton and Julia's fingers, but because the wreath had to be pushed hastily under her bed every time she heard footsteps on the stairs.

It was finished by bedtime. That is, all the flowers were used up, but it did not look very much like one of Mr Bound's wreaths, it was so thin and bedraggled, and the wood of the hoop showed through. With eyes aching from peering at black cotton, a crick in her neck and her back, she flung the wreath under the bed. She had no idea what she was going to do with it now, all she wanted was to read a bit of *The Dove in the Eagle's Nest* before it was time to go to bed.

'Did you manage to make the wreath?' Henry asked her next morning.

'Gracious!' Julia put her hand to her mouth in horror. 'It's under my bed and I can hear Ellen sweeping out the bedroom now.'

She galloped up the stairs and flung herself into the bedroom. But she was too late, the wreath had been discovered and lay on the bed, looking rather worse than it did yesterday. The flowers were limper, and they had picked up a lot of white fluff from under the bed.

'I was just a coming to ask you what this was, Miss Julia.'

'It's only a sort of game. Could I have it now, Ellen?'

'A fine thing to keep under your bed. And where did those bits of flowers come from, may I ask?'

'I bought them,' said Julia defensively.

'Well if you choose to spend your money on flowers and then put them under your bed it's no business of mine, though there's many a poor family that would be glad of that money. And remember those that have got to keep your room clean next time you're thinking of putting rubbish under your bed.' Ellen was in a very snappy mood that morning.

Furtively trying to hide the wreath behind her back, Julia ran down to the schoolroom. Amy, who was dressing one of her dolls, looked at the wilting pansies with disdain.

'Is that the wreath you made? Doesn't it look queer. Couldn't you have bought more alive flowers than that?'

'Shall I dust some of the fluff off and tie up the cotton?' said Henry more tactfully.

Julia knew how odd the wreath looked, but all this made her feel thoroughly irritable, even with Henry who was doing his best.

'No, you needn't bother, I'm in a hurry. I'm going to take it to Westminster Abbey now.' Until this very minute she had not decided any such thing. She hoped Henry and Amy would look appalled at this announcement, but they took it very calmly.

'You will be back in time for dinner, won't you?' Henry begged. 'I don't expect anybody will notice you're not here till then, but I don't know what I'll say then.'

'I'll do my best,' Julia said grandly. 'But you'll have to come with me if Kate can't.' She did not wait to see what effect this announcement had on Henry, but walked haughtily out of the room. It seemed as though events had taken charge of her, and that she was being swept along in spite of herself. 'Perhaps,' she thought with rising excitement, 'this is destiny sweeping me along, and I am going to be great!'

She threw on her coat and hat, snatched up what was left of the money from her money-box, picked up the wreath and marched downstairs. She could hear her mother's voice in the kitchen; she was discussing the menus for the day with Mabel, and secure now that she would not be seen, Julia let herself out of the front door.

As she turned in at the Holts' gate, a little uneasy now, and wondering what she was going to say to whoever opened the door, destiny came to her rescue again. She heard the distant bounce of a ball from the Holts' backyard, and walked up in that direction. Kate was there, standing on one foot and bouncing a ball against the wall.

'You'll have to wait till I've done this seven times,' she said, hardly bothering to look at Julia. But she never reached seven; she was just counting five and wobbling

precariously on her left foot when Richard appeared
through the gate that led into the backyard from the
garden.

'Woggle, I have tried to endure the monotonous thud
thud, but I am afraid I cannot any longer. I happen to
be composing a set of hexameters for Mr James.' He
still held a pen in his hand, his fingers were extremely
inky, and there was ink on his forehead. Then he noticed
Julia.

'Mercy, who have we here? A young lady in walking
costume?'

Julia tried to be as dignified as she could. 'I just came
to say that I'm going to Westminster Abbey now.'

'To Westminster Abbey!' Richard chewed his pen,
already bitten to splinters at its end. 'You mean you are
going to Byron's tomb?'

'Yes, and I've got the wreath.' However, she tried to
hide it behind her back.

'Well, well. If that is the case I had better abandon
Mr James' hexameters and come with you. Go and
groom thyself, Woggle, we are all going to London.'

Julia waited with the wreath while they went into the
house. When they came out Kate was carrying Monarch
in her arms. Richard followed her benevolently, most
of the ink washed off his face, though a little still
remained on his forehead.

'Note Woggle's gloves,' he remarked. 'Donned in
honour of you. She models herself on you Greshams.
Poor Woggle, she yearns to be respectable. Though I
must say, the respectability of your appearance today is
somewhat marred by the object you are carrying.'

The wreath certainly did look odder than ever in the
open. Julia had not managed to brush off all the fluff,
the flowers, all of them, were limp and faded, and
many of them had slipped. It was also difficult to know
how to carry it. The only comfortable way was to wear

it like a gigantic bracelet on her arm.

'Still,' Richard said comfortingly. 'What does it matter? The great thing is the attitude of mind. Yours is much better than I dared hope. Have you got a book for the journey? Well, you'd better come and choose one.'

In a glow of pleasure at Richard's praise, Julia followed him into the house. He took her to the study and waved his hand towards the walls of books. 'Any of these. The classics on your right, history in front of you, poetry on your left, theology behind.'

There was no time to pick and choose and consider. Julia advanced towards the poetry shelves, saw a red morocco volume of Byron in front of her and hastily took out that. It would be just as well to know something about the man she was supposed to be paying homage to.

They walked briskly down Station road. Julia could not think of anything clever enough to say to Richard, and besides, she was nervously conscious of how odd they must all look; Richard inky and hatless, Kate in a coat that was far too bright a blue, and carrying Monarch, and above all, the miserable wreath. She kept close to the wall and held it in her inside hand. In the end Richard noticed.

'You poor Greshams,' he remarked. 'Always worrying about what people think. And here's Woggle, who would like to be a Gresham more than anything else in the world—until she becomes a duchess. Little does she know what agony it is to be a Gresham. Do you, Woggle?' But Kate, with a bright red face, only muttered something that could not be heard. 'Hold your head up,' Richard went on to Julia. 'You're going to be great, aren't you? If people are going to notice you, give them something to notice so that they can say to their grandchildren that they saw Julia Gresham walking down the High street.'

Julia hated Richard talking like this; she never knew whether he was joking or not. But she did try to be less self-conscious and forget about the wreath. She had more respect for Richard than anybody else she had ever met, and longed to win his good opinion.

In the train he sat absorbed in his book. It was volume five of Gibbon's *Decline and Fall of the Roman Empire*, Julia noticed. She was always very interested in what other people were reading, and longed for them to be as interested in her own books. She felt too excited to give much attention to Byron, however, and kept looking up and eyeing Richard and Kate. She caught Richard's eye at last.

'Look at Woggle,' he remarked. 'She is Catherine Mary Jocelyn, Duchess of What Have You, riding to Court in her carriage.'

Kate, who was sitting bolt upright, gazing out of the window with a rapt expression on her face, and bowing and raising her hand from time to time, came out of her dream and flung herself on Richard, trying to hold her hands over his mouth.

'Or was it Catherine Mary Jocelyn riding to hounds followed by an adoring throng?' said Richard in a muffled voice between Kate's fingers. Julia, who had constantly been told by her parents that no lady ever even raised her voice in a railway carriage, watched with amazement.

They walked out of the bustle of Victoria station, where engine whistles were shrieking and people were bumping and jostling, into the station yard outside. There Julia stopped. For the first time since they had started out, a sense of the outrageousness of what she was doing came over her. Here she was, alone in London except for some children she hardly knew, with not the remotest idea of where Westminster Abbey was

or how she was going to get there. She stared hopelessly
at the omnibuses that were drawn up a little way off.

'Well?' said Richard.

'I don't know where the Abbey is or anything,' she
said desperately. 'Papa did once take Henry and me
there, but it was a long time ago when we were quite
small and I think we must have gone in a cab.'

'Let's take a cab,' said Kate. 'Oh do let's. Aunt B
gave me three shillings and I've still got two shillings
left. I've always wanted to go in one.'

'A hansom?' Julia was so completely taken by surprise
that she forgot Richard's scorn for Greshams who
worried about what people thought. The Holts turned
to stare at her. She felt they expected her to explain. 'I
mean I thought ladies didn't go in hansoms alone, that
is without their fathers or people,' she faltered miserably.

'We shall go in a hansom, Woggle,' said Richard with
authority.

They did take a cab. Kate's excited beckonings
brought one, though not the one she wanted with the
smart chestnut horse. Once inside, Kate sat counting
her money anxiously, Monarch on her knee.

'Will threepence be enough for the tip?' she said
anxiously. 'I know you have to give cabmen tips but I
want to tell him that twopence of it is for the horse. Do
you think I can?'

'Speaking for myself, Woggle,' remarked Richard. 'I
think on the whole I would not. But you must please
yourself.'

Kate sat and thought about this and seemed to pay no
attention to the crowded street and the shops that the
cab was passing. Finally she clenched her fists and said
determinedly, 'I will. It can't do any harm.' She was
so eager to get on with it that when the cab finally
stopped she leapt out before either of the others, thrust
the money up at the man and with a scarlet face said,

'Tuppence of that is for your horse.'

'Cor,' remarked the cabby, grinning hugely, 'get him shod in gold next time he wants new shoes.' Then he peered down inside. 'Left somethin' behind, haven't you?'

It was the unfortunate wreath, and blushing, Julia went back to collect it. As she shamefacedly tried to conceal it under her arm, Richard looked at her.

'Take a lesson from Woggle. She's going to be a duchess, and duchesses simply don't care a fig for what people think. If they want to give tuppence to a cab-horse they do. Hold your wreath in front of you and try to be great.'

Blinking nervously and glad she could not see all the hundreds of people who seemed to be strolling past the Abbey in the September sun, Julia marched behind Richard, holding the wreath as unconcernedly as she knew how. They caught up Kate outside the door.

'You'll have to go in by yourselves. Monarch and I will stay here.'

'Yes, I am afraid that even a wolfhound of the bluest blood would be frowned upon in the Abbey,' Richard remarked. 'We'll try to be as quick as we can, but it really depends on how long Julia takes paying her respects to Byron.'

He pushed Julia in through the great door. It was dim inside, and there was a hushed murmur as though the huge building was filled with people trying to move stealthily and speak in whispers. But Julia's first feeling was one of great dismay. There were tombs every-where, even the walls were lined with memorial tablets clustered as thickly as the books in Mr Holt's study. However was she going to find Byron's? She peered round her shortsightedly, and then timidly asked Richard.

'When in doubt ask a policeman,' said Richard

serenely. 'I shall wait for you here.' He sat down in one of the chairs arranged for the congregation, and closed his eyes reverently.

Julia looked at him in despair and reflected that she could hardly disturb him now. She drifted hopelessly on, and found herself walking down by the side of the part of the Abbey where the choir sat. The carved choir stalls looked far more interesting than the tombs, but there was no time to loiter and look now. She hurried on saying to herself that she would look only at the really big, important tombs, because surely Byron would be given something better than a stone in the wall. But to her horrified consternation she found herself standing in a part of the Abbey where there seemed to be nothing else but big, important tombs. There they were, ranged side by side, tightly jammed together like the turkeys in the poulterer's at Christmas. As far as you could see there were white stone figures standing on top of tombs and making sweeping gestures. Even if she only looked at these it would take her a whole day. And beyond this transept she could still see the Abbey stretching, apparently limitless; quite obviously she had not seen a tenth of it yet.

She was roused from her despair by the murmuring of female voices near her and the clattering of many feet. Feeling rather confused at being found standing about like this (Captain Gresham had taught them that there was something very ill-bred about loitering), she looked round and saw a man in a black gown advancing on her; he seemed to have an air of authority. She hastily made her way over to him.

'If you please,' she said, clutching the wreath behind her back. 'Can you tell me where Byron's tomb is?'

'Byron?' said the man haughtily, looking her up and down. 'You'll have to look again, miss. We don't have the likes of *him* here.'

Too late she realized that he was conducting a party of ladies. They halted behind him and looked at her curiously. 'Fancy a little girl asking for a man like that,' said a stout woman loudly, clucking her tongue. The women with her murmured, and one of them stepped forward and took Julia by the arm.

'Little girl,' she said in an earnest voice, 'are you by yourself? Do you think your mother would like it? Why not come with us? We are the Ladies' Bright Hour from Putney, and we will make you one of us for the morning.'

Julia was horrified, and hardly knew what she was saying. 'Thank you very much,' she stammered at last. 'My friends are waiting for me. I think I'd better go.'

She felt she could not run in a church, but as fast as she could she walked. She passed splendid tombs, little chapels with rich stonework and colour, but she did not dare look or turn her head in case the Ladies' Bright Hour caught her up and tried to adopt her again. Ahead of her lay a flight of steps. She pounded up them and found herself at last at the end of the Abbey in a place more splendid than any of the rest. After the dimness she had emerged from, it seemed bathed in light, and even the stone looked whiter. Down both sides of the chapel, over the carved stalls that lined them, hung gorgeous coloured banners. But even here the Ladies' Bright Hour might catch her up. Greatly daring, Julia edged into one of the stalls and sank down on her knees. In this position she was hidden by the high desk in front, and anyway, surely they would not disturb her if they thought she was saying her prayers? She pressed her knuckles into her eyes until stars jumped in the blackness.

'Do let me be great,' she started praying, 'and be buried here. Show me what I've got to do to be great. Let people remember me after I'm dead.'

She relaxed the pressure of her knuckles and peered
through her fingers at the stalls and banners opposite.
From far down in the body of the Abbey the organ suddenly sounded, very solemn and grand, and she felt

moved almost to tears. How wonderful it must be to have a right to sit here; she wondered whether she would ever know anybody who did. Henry did not really have the stuff of greatness in him, but perhaps Richard . . .

Then she became suddenly conscious of the passing of time. She had left Richard for hours and hours, and Kate outside, holding Monarch. She jumped to her feet, and as she did the wretched hoop clattered down on the floor beside her. Her despair came back. Byron was not here, she had failed in the task she had been set. But then inspiration poured into her. What did it matter if Byron was not actually buried here. She could leave it as a tribute to his memory just as well, and as a tribute as well to all the greatness that lay buried around her. She would leave the wreath in this very spot. No longer furtive, but with calm dignity, she picked a few last bits of fluff off the pansies, propped the wreath against the back of the stall where she had been sitting, and walked away, more pleased with herself than she had ever felt before.

CHAPTER 6

Henry Fails

Julia came back from Westminster Abbey in a trance of happiness, not noticing where she was going, what she was doing. Victoria street seemed full of a golden September sunshine, and she wanted to stop the people that thronged it and shake them by the hand. She could not do that, so she walked with her shoulders flung back and her head held high, hoping that she would be noticed. For her task was accomplished; even Richard had commended her for the way she had carried it out, and she was going to be great, she felt certain of it now. She jostled into people, twice or three times Richard had to drag her out of the way of a passing cab, but she neither noticed nor cared. When they got back again to Victoria Kate stopped them near the ticket office and started fumbling with coins in her pocket.

'Darling, darling Richard, can you lend me sixpence? Just this once. I'll pay it back as soon as Aunt B gives me some more.' She clung on to his arm and looked at him beseechingly.

'Steady, Woggle, we are not alone.' Richard removed her arm from his sleeve and straightened it. 'Besides, why should you want sixpence? You must have got some money left from the cab.'

'Well, you see,' Kate started hesitatingly, and then went on with a rush. 'I want to change our tickets for first-class ones. You see I've always wanted to go into a first-class carriage and I haven't ever, and it wouldn't cost so very much more just for such a little way. Oh Richard, please, please, I want to so much that it hurts.'

'I can see that it does, poor Woggle, there are tears in

your eyes. Very well, here is your sixpence. Only I must have it back, mind.'

Kate darted off. She came back more slowly. 'There wasn't enough to make them into first-class tickets, so I've made them into second-class ones. It's not the same of course, but it is a bit better.'

'Sixpence gone west to gratify Woggle's vanity,' remarked Richard. 'Come along, it's platform seven.'

Kate gave a little squeal of delight when they got to platform seven. 'Look, the train goes on to Fareham. That's where Christ's is. Perhaps there'll be some Christ's boys on the train.'

'There will not,' Richard told her calmly. 'The winter half does not start for a week yet, so curb your enthusiasm, Woggle mine.'

'Well, there's one anyway,' retorted Kate. 'That's you. You're as good as one.'

Richard made no reply to this, and Kate left him and went to peer disconsolately into the windows of the first-class carriages. 'It's one like that I want to go in. Richard, do let me one day.' She pointed to a carriage that was furnished like a drawing-room, with armchairs and sofas arranged round it. It was occupied by one red-faced man in a bright check suit who was smoking a cigar. 'And I'd get out all smelling of cigars—it would be wonderful.'

'It would be most improper,' Richard told her. 'You wouldn't be fit company for any little Greshams then.'

The second-class carriage that they got into had no one in it, rather to Julia's disappointment. True, the seats were more comfortable, but she too had hoped that by changing their tickets they would gain interesting people to travel with, and if there was not to be anybody it was hardly worth changing. Kate bore the disappointment well, and within a few seconds of settling herself had obviously, by her rapt expression, gone into the dream world where she was a duchess.

Just before the train left somebody did get into the carriage. Julia out of the corner of her eye saw a lady in a brown cloak. She settled herself beside Julia, who instantly judged that she might be more interesting than the sort of lady in her mother's circle of friends, who never came back from London without a cluster of parcels from the Army and Navy Stores, or from Gorringe's. And when this lady opened her reticule and produced some papers which she then proceeded to rustle and look through, Julia felt thoroughly excited and hopeful. Why, she might even be an authoress. This would be the moment to produce her book and show that she read poetry. She opened it at random and with her heart thumping loudly in her ears let her eyes travel over the print—she did not see what she was reading. She was conscious at last of the lady by her side taking an interest, of reading over her shoulder, in fact. But she did not raise her eyes, she turned over a page from time to time, and put on an expression of ferocious concentration. This seemed to go on for about an hour—though the journey to Melsham only took fifteen minutes. At last she could tell by the sound of the train going into a tunnel that they were nearly there, and with a sigh that she hoped sounded genuine, she closed the book of Byron. The lady next to her spoke at last.

'And what book have you there?'

Julia tried to speak as casually as she could. 'It's Lord Byron's poems. I was just reading *Don Juan*.' (By a lucky chance she remembered the title that ran across the top of the pages.)

'May I ask whether your mother knows that you read Byron's verse? And does she usually allow you to travel alone in railway carriages?'

Stunned by the unexpectedness of this remark, Julia

looked up at the lady in brown. She saw at once that she had made a terrible mistake, this person could not possibly be interested in poetry; she was thin, wrinkled, severe, and wore pince-nez. At this point Kate broke in, bristling with indignation.

'She's not alone, she's with me and my brother. We've been doing perfectly respectable things, we've been to Westminster Abbey in a hansom cab, and Richard lent her that book she's reading. I don't know what it is, but it's sure to be good, because it's Father's.'

The lady in brown turned her pince-nez on Kate and Richard and looked them up and down with pointed disapproval, marking, Julia thought, the ink on Richard's face, Kate's untidy hair and the holes in her gloves, and the dirty toy dog that she was carrying.

'I see,' she said, and drew on her gloves. The train drew in at Melsham station; the lady gathered up her belongings, gave Julia another severe glance, and stepped out.

'I can't bear people prying and poking their noses into things that don't concern them,' said Kate in a loud and challenging voice that was intended to carry.

'So much for your second-class carriage, Woggle,' remarked Richard, stepping out behind her. 'Poor Julia, it was rather unfortunate that she should choose to read *Don Juan* next to somebody who belonged to Our Girls Welfare and Rescue Crusade. Obviously she now thinks that Julia needs rescuing too.'

'How do you know that she belongs to that?' Julia demanded feverishly.

'And what's wrong with what Julia was reading, anyway? It's one of Father's books, isn't it?' Kate was red with indignation.

'To answer your questions one at a time. I saw she was reading a report of the Crusade's work. It was on her lap, I have good eyesight and I can read upside down. As regards *Don Juan*, quite a lot of people consider it improper and that young girls should be protected against it. What makes it all a little unfortunate is that the good lady appears to know Julia.'

This was a horror that had not yet occurred to Julia. 'She can't do, she would have said. Anyway, it's not fair, I'd never heard of *Don Juan* until this very minute, and I can't remember a word of what it's about, anyway.' In her anguish she did not bother to keep up the pretence of having literary tastes.

'She can't know Julia. Julia was staring at her hard enough and *she* doesn't know who she was,' said Kate.

'But I never know anybody,' wailed Julia. 'I just can't recognize people. Oh, I do hope it wasn't anybody who knows me.'

'There she is, walking up in front of you.' Kate pointed out a figure in a brown cloak walking briskly up Station road. 'Don't you know now?'

Julia screwed up her eyes and poked her head forward, trying to see through the mist that for her always shrouded distant objects. 'No, I don't know. All sorts of people seem to know me when I don't know them.'

'Don't brood on it,' Richard advised her. 'Think how much you've broadened your horizons today.'

So Julia tried to return to that blissful state of triumph. But it was more difficult in Station road, Westminster Abbey seemed far away. They were all silent until they turned into Clifton road.

'Hullo,' said Richard. 'There's your brother and your little sister. They look a bit lost. Do you suppose they're worrying about you? I shouldn't have thought young Amy could worry about anybody.'

Henry had seen them too. He came hurrying down, dragging Amy behind him. 'Oh Ju, I'm so glad you've come back. It's been hours.'

'Why, is it past dinnertime? Are they looking for me?'

'No, I don't think anybody's noticed yet. But we've just seen the Old Dame.'

'Keep calm,' said Richard. 'Soldiers have to be calm, surely. Anyway, she's been safe with me and Woggle, to say nothing of Woggle's faithful bodyguard, Monarch.'

'Henry wasn't calm when the Old Dame passed,' Amy announced. 'He ran away. Into Dr Watson's back gate. I didn't run, I stayed. She said did Mamma know I was there and I said no she didn't.'

'That's what the person in the train said to Julia,' Richard said calmly. ' "Does your mother know you're here?" Perhaps it was the same person.'

A cold horror went through Julia. 'When did you see the Old Dame? Just now? Was she wearing a brown cloak?'

Amy stared at her. 'Of course she was, she always does. Fancy not knowing the Old Dame. You've seen her often enough in her garden.'

'But I wasn't expecting to see her,' Julia wailed. 'I mean I always think of her in her garden, not in trains.'

Richard seemed amused. 'And who is this Old Dame who strikes terror into you all? Dear me, what a chicken-hearted lot you are.'

Stung by this, Julia tried to appear calm and indifferent again. But Henry was white to the lips. 'She's dreadful. She has the house behind our back garden—you know, the one Mrs Vonnister went into—and she's always complaining and writing notes about us to Mamma, and putting her head over the wall to tell us to be quiet.'

Richard went into cackles of laughter. 'And now Mrs Vonnister has gone down her chimney. There's justice for you! But soldiers shouldn't worry about trifles like Old Dames, should they?'

Henry's lips trembled at this, and he walked very forlornly up Clifton road beside Julia, with hanging head. He hated being teased or scolded, and this sounded painfully like something his father might have said. Richard turned round and noticed.

'Poor Henry is easily cast down. We must do something for him like we have done for Julia. Report to me in the conservatory at five-thirty this evening and we will see if we cannot make you more worthy of the Society for Achieving Greatness.' He lifted his hand in farewell and pushed open the gate of number 24. Kate followed.

Apparently nobody had noticed Julia's absence. She was determined not to show any signs of weakness to Henry, but all the same, she was rather apprehensive as she walked into the house. There was a sound of dishes being clattered about in the scullery, but otherwise the house was quiet and there seemed to be nobody raging round looking for her. She tiptoed upstairs to take off her outdoor clothes, then came down and opened the kitchen door. On a checked cloth the table was laid for the maids' dinner, and Mabel was stooping in front of the range pulling something out of the oven. She turned a hot red face over her shoulder. 'Go away, Miss Julia, there's a good girl. Your dinner won't be more than a few minutes now. I'm sure I'm just as hungry as you are.'

Nothing about 'you naughty girl, where have you been?' Greatly relieved, Julia went upstairs and got ready for dinner. It was mutton stew today, she knew by the smell. Ellen beat the gong and then brought the stew, the mashed turnip and the potatoes into the dining-room. Mrs Gresham came downstairs in her hat with the red cherries on it. Tuesday afternoon was the day she paid calls.

'Say grace Amy dear,' she said when she had glanced

round the table at the three children to see that their
hair was tidy and Amy's pinafore clean. It was quite
plain that nobody had noticed Julia's absence; she
became light-hearted and even forgot to mind about
the mutton stew which she usually detested because
of the barley. The only thing that was irritating was
Henry's behaviour. He looked white-faced and distressed,
and toyed with his food. Julia avoided him after dinner
and went and shut herself up in the bedroom with
Westward Ho! Novels were allowed after dinner, and
though her mother did not approve of her reading in the
bedroom she was going to be out all afternoon, paying
calls. It would be best to keep away from Henry while
he was in this worrying mood, and *Westward Ho!* was
the thing to keep her from dwelling on the Old Dame
and what she might be going to do. She sat on the floor
with the book and propped her back against the chest of
drawers. She tried to banish her nagging uneasiness by
reasoning with herself. In the first place it might not
have been the Old Dame in the train. But this was not
much comfort, she was fairly certain that it could have
been nobody else. In the second place, she had no reason
at all to go round complaining about Julia. It was not
like making a noise, or throwing balls into her garden,
or standing on her wall, Julia had just been in a train
doing no harm to anybody. How could she come round
to Clifton road and complain about that? This was a
very good line of reasoning, it convinced Julia and
comforted her, and after that she buried herself in
Westward Ho! and gave nothing else a thought.

She was disturbed at last, long afterwards, by Amy
bursting into the room in a great state of excitement.

'I thought you'd be here. Henry's been sick—all his
mutton stew. He's finished now, he's in the schoolroom.
And do you know why it was? It's because he looked out
of the bathroom window and saw Mamma, sitting in the

Old Dame's drawing-room. The sun was shining through the net curtains and you could see Mamma's hat with the red cherries. I expect she's telling Mamma all about you on the train with the Holts. Henry was so frightened that it made him sick. Shall I tell Mamma to give him some Syrup of Figs when she comes back?'

'You can do what you like,' snapped Julia. She was frightened too, and it made her angry. 'But go away now, I want to read.'

'Mamma doesn't like you reading in the bedroom. Anyway, it's nearly teatime so you'll have to come.'

When she went down, Julia found Henry lolling listlessly in the brown plush chair in the schoolroom. He looked extremely pale, and there were dark circles round his eyes. Julia glanced at him without much sympathy; Henry was always having headaches or being sick.

'Ju, what are we going to do?' he moaned. 'The Old Dame will have told Mamma everything now, and Mamma will tell Papa as soon as he comes home and there'll be a most awful row and we'll be stopped from ever seeing the Holts again.'

'I don't see how you're helping matters by being sick,' Julia said crossly. 'Anyway, it probably wasn't Mamma at all that you saw, I looked out of the window and couldn't see anything.' (While she was in the bathroom, washing her hands, she had clambered up on the mahogany casing of the bath to peer through the window. But the sun had gone in by this time and the lace curtains of the Old Dame's drawing-room were impenetrable.) 'Or were you sick because you're afraid of what Richard's going to tell you to do after tea?'

'I do feel rather awful,' pleaded Henry. 'Not like playing.'

'It isn't playing, it's serious. Do try and be a bit more like a soldier, like Richard said.'

G.G.   D

Mrs Gresham did not come in to tea. On her calling day she was usually out until six or so, and they always had tea in the kitchen with the maids. This usually was a treat, Ellen would talk about her young man who was in the tanning business (he worked in the tannery at the other end of Melsham; it smelt dreadful, but you caught fascinating glimpses of dark pools if the gates happened to be open). And Mabel would tell fortunes with the tea-leaves in her cup, and sometimes could be persuaded to try to remember the book on palmistry she had once read and tell their fortunes from their hands.

But tea today was very silent. Julia felt apprehensive and ill-tempered and was wondering how long it would be before her mother came back. Henry drooped over his plate, and was still nibbling at his first, jamless, piece of bread and butter when Amy had reached the cake stage.

'Well, we are sunny and bright today and no mistake,' said Mabel at last. None of them, except perhaps Amy, had taken the slightest interest in the tall dark stranger with one shoulder higher than another that Mabel had predicted from the curiously shaped tea-leaf she had found in her cup. 'There's no use talking if folks won't talk. You'd better say grace, Miss Amy, and run off all of you. I've got starching to do.'

Julia went back into the bedroom and shut the door. At half-past five she emerged again and marched into the schoolroom. Amy looked up from her dolls.

'Henry says he's still feeling sick, but he hasn't been, I know, because I've been here all the time.'

'Have I got to go?' said Henry faintly. Then he added hopefully, 'Perhaps I oughtn't to go until Mamma comes back and gives me some medicine.'

'Mamma's going to be so angry with me, according to you, that she surely won't have time to give you medicine,' Julia said caustically. 'Come along, we're late.'

Henry dragged himself to his feet. He was actually shivering, Julia noticed. Outside number 24 he clutched her arm.

'Ju, do you think he'll make me go to Westminster Abbey too? I just couldn't, it's no good.'

'Are you frightened of Richard?' Amy said incredulously. 'I'm not. I'll go and see if he's in the conservatory.' She ran on ahead and came skipping back over the gravel. 'Yes, he's there. He's reading—just like Julia.'

Julia gave him an impatient little push. 'Go on, then. Don't be so stupid, he won't hurt you.' But she felt a guilty pang as she watched him slink off. A moment later Kate appeared round the corner of the house. She had a piece of bread and jam in one hand and was licking the fingers of the other.

'Hullo. What's wrong with Henry?'

'He's been sick. A lot,' said Amy with relish. She eyed the bread and jam with disapproval. 'Why are you eating out of doors?'

'Because we've been having tea in the garden, that's why, Miss Nosey Parker. You'd better come round to the back. Father's in the study and I don't want to disturb him.'

She led the way round the far side of the house, into the backyard, and out into the garden. 'We're not going past the conservatory because Richard doesn't like people poking and prying at him,' she remarked to Amy.

'I don't poke and pry,' Amy said virtuously.

'I'd like to know what you're doing all the time at that window with the bars across it, then. Staring at us like that.'

'I don't stare. I just look out, that's all. I can't help it if you're in the garden when I'm doing it, can I?'

'Can't you just!' Kate gave a sarcastic laugh, put the last piece of bread into her mouth so that her cheek bulged, and then sat herself down on a makeshift swing that somebody had hung from one of the lowest branches of the apple tree—a loop of rope with a battered cushion for the seat. She swung herself backwards and forwards, scraping her feet over the trampled earth of the flower-bed below; it was impossible to swing much because of the fence behind.

'Richard won't keep him long; he wants to read,' she observed. 'If that's what you're worrying about.'

'We aren't worrying.' Amy was indignant. 'It's only Henry, he always does. He was sick.'

'So you keep saying. Anyway, here he is.'

Julia looked anxiously in the direction of the conservatory. You never knew with Henry, he could get himself so frightened that he might actually faint—there was the time he had fallen like a stone to the floor of the dentist's waiting room, for instance. But to her short-sighted eyes he looked almost cheerful.

'Richard says I've got to climb the apple tree,' he called.

Behind him Richard came strolling along, his finger in a book, his face creased with thought. Julia recognized his expression; it meant he wanted to get on with his book and would be impatient of any interruptions. 'I'll leave you to it,' he said to Henry. 'When you're up I'll come out and see.' He disappeared into the house.

Henry was quite gay with relief. 'It's nothing difficult at all. I thought he'd make me go to London. But the apple tree's easy, I've always wanted to climb it anyway.'

Henry walked up to the tree and surveyed it. It was a large tree, and its lowest branches started some eight feet or so from the ground, but on the other hand it stood only about a foot away from the fence, so that if you could climb on to that you would be in a position to attack the tree. Henry had worked this out the first time he had seen the tree from the Holts' garden.

'What I need is a box or something,' he said in a businesslike way.

'There's one in the shed.' Kate sat on her swing and pushed herself backwards and forwards. 'Two if you want them.'

Henry bustled between the tree and the shed, bringing out boxes, measuring them against the fence, putting them on top of one another and testing them for strength.

'Oh hurry,' said Amy. 'It'll be my bedtime soon and they'll start looking for us.'

This thought goaded Henry into action. He stepped on to the first box, climbed on to the second, balanced on it, and from there scrambled on to the fence. The vast privet hedge on the Greshams' side reared itself four or five feet higher than the fence, and Henry held on to it while he examined the apple tree and considered what branch would provide the best starting point.

'You're being so slow,' complained Amy, hopping about impatiently. 'Shall I come up too?'

At this point they heard Ellen calling from the other garden. 'Miss A-mee, your bedtime. Come along, there's a good girl.'

Amy stopped hopping and froze into stillness. Henry gave a nervous start, and crouched down on the fence behind the hedge. Ellen's voice came nearer. 'Drat that child,' they heard her say irritably. Amy giggled and pressed her hands to her mouth. 'Miss Amy, Miss Amy. Your pa's come home and there'll be trouble if you don't come at once.' There was a pause, then they heard her feet going away, up the steps into the house. Amy stopped giggling and looked thoughtful.

'Do you think Papa really is come home? He never does come as early as this usually.'

Henry looked down from the fence with a horror-stricken face. 'Ju, we must go. Now. Papa's home. Quickly, move those boxes to me so that I can get down.'

But Julia did not get there in time. From the window of the girls' bedroom came Mrs Gresham's voice.

'Amy, whatever do you think you are doing in that garden? And what do you mean by not answering Ellen when she called you. Come in this instant, you naughty girl.'

'Oh Mamma,' wailed Amy. 'Just a few more minutes. Henry's climbing the tree, and I do want to see him get up but he's so slow.'

Then came Captain Gresham's voice from inside the room. 'What, Henry climbing a tree? What tree?'

Amy rushed over to the tree. 'It's Papa,' she announced. 'I can see him standing there. You'd better hurry, Henry.'

Henry clung limply to the hedge, looking as though he

was trying to bury himself in the privet. 'Can he see me?' he said desperately.

Of course he meant that he hoped that Captain Gresham could not see him, but Amy chose to misunderstand.

'Henry says can you see him, Papa? He's standing on the fence holding on to the hedge.'

Captain Gresham threw up the window and craned out over the bars. 'Yes, I can see him. What are you doing there, Henry? If you're going to climb the tree, climb it.'

But Henry, seemingly frightened out of the use of his limbs, only clutched the privet harder. An uneasy silence fell on them all. Amy got impatient. 'Oh Henry, it's so easy. I'll show you.' Before anybody could stop her she was scrambling up the boxes.

'Amy!' said her mother, horrified. 'Get down at once, you naughty girl. What do you think you're doing. You'll fall.'

'She won't fall,' said Captain Gresham. 'That girl's got spirit. Not like her brother, I'm sorry to say. Call yourself a man, Henry, and you stand there snivelling like that while your baby sister climbs a tree. Not much of the soldier spirit in *you*!'

This praise intoxicated Amy, as well as the feeling that everybody was watching her. She crawled up on to the fence beside Henry, with a face bright red from her efforts, and said triumphantly, 'Look at me where I am.' Then she turned a little, hesitated, and put one foot into the fork where the branches started. Very daringly, she let go her hold of the hedge and swung herself up into the tree.

'Bravo, Amy, that's my brave girl,' Captain Gresham called. 'That's sixpence for you. Henry, I'm disgusted with you. You ought to be ashamed.'

'And you're all just coming along back home with me

this minute, that's your ma's orders.' Ellen, red-faced and angry, came panting up the path by the greenhouse. 'Why couldn't you answer when I called you? Giving me all this trouble of coming in and fetching you. And my word, I wouldn't be in your shoes, Miss Julia and Master Henry. There's trouble coming to you. What it's about is not my business, but I can tell from your pa's look that you're in for a bad time.'

CHAPTER 7

Dressing-Rooms and Cellars

They all went back with Ellen. Amy skipped ahead, elated by the thought of the sixpence and by her father's approval. Julia marched beside Ellen, trying to appear unmoved, as befitted someone who that morning had taken the first steps towards greatness. But Henry crept along behind them all, far too miserable even to try to keep up appearances in front of the Holts: Kate, who sat on her swing, staring at them open-mouthed, Richard who had come to the garden door with a mild expression of surprise on his face. Henry dreaded his father's anger more than anything else in the world, and there was no comfort in thinking that this time Julia was going to get most of it because of her escapade in London. Captain Gresham's anger was terrible, whoever received it, and it made Henry feel ill for days afterwards.

As they were going in through the back door Julia turned and saw Henry. 'I don't know why you're looking like a dying duck,' she said snappishly. 'It's me he's going to be angry with.'

'As far as I can see you're all in it together, Miss Julia,' said Ellen, overhearing. 'For one thing your pa won't like you playing with those children. (And whoever gave you permission to go creeping off into their garden, I'd like to know? I certainly didn't, and I'll tell your pa so if he asks.) And for another, why couldn't you come when you were called? Disobedience is a thing that makes the Captain really wild, and quite right too.'

'Papa's not going to be angry with me,' Amy stated confidently. 'I climbed the tree and Henry couldn't. He's going to give me sixpence.'

Unfortunately Amy was right. Mabel looked up from the little rolls of starched clothes on the kitchen table.

'The Captain wants to see Miss Julia and Master Henry in the dressing-room straight away. No, he didn't say anything about you, Miss Amy, though I'm sure you deserve it as richly as anyone, knowing you.' And as the children went out of the kitchen, Julia heard Mabel saying in undertones to Ellen. 'My word, the Captain's put out this evening and no mistake. You should have seen the look he gave me just because I took a minute or two to answer the dressing-room bell. I was up to my eyes in the starching, I couldn't get there any quicker. But my word, black looks weren't in it, I can tell you.'

Captain Gresham was indeed in a bad humour. He had had to leave the office early to come home to dress. He and Mrs Gresham were going out to dinner with people whom he profoundly disliked, but worse than this he detested the way it upset the day's routine. Then as soon as he got home his wife had met him with some incoherent story about Julia and a railway station, which had been interrupted by Ellen, who complained that Amy was nowhere to be found. Amy was soon found, they heard her voice in the next door garden, but what did he see when he looked out of the window but Henry behaving as though he were not a Gresham at all— Henry, a boy of ten who was going to be a soldier, afraid to climb a tree!

He interviewed Henry and Julia together in the dressing-room, striding up and down angrily trying to put the studs into his stiff shirt (which Henry could never believe was not made of cardboard, it was so rigid and gleaming). The walls of the dressing-room were hung three deep with framed photographs of regimental groups, and of men wearing topees standing round shot tigers, or reclining, supported by their elbows, at what seemed to be croquet or lawn tennis parties. The room smelt of tobacco and tweed and boot polish, and Henry hated it; he had always associated it with his father's severest manner, and with the slippering he had once had as a small boy for scribbling on the walls of his bedroom.

Julia saw Henry's lips moving as they went up the stairs, and she knew that he was saying to himself over and over again in a frenzy 'Lord, in Thee have I trusted, let me never be confounded.' It was his talisman in times of trouble; once, in a burst of confidence he had admitted to her that he always said it before his boxing lessons, and if he had to play football with bigger boys. What a coward Henry was, she thought angrily, it was she that he ought to be worrying about; never in all the history of the family had one of the children done anything so outrageously daring as running off to London and travelling in a hansom into the bargain.

But Julia was wrong. Captain Gresham paid her no attention; he was completely taken up with disgust at how Henry had behaved, and how useless it was to talk to him about the Gresham family tradition. Afraid to climb a tree, and this in front of strangers! All the same, he did talk about it for what seemed to be an hour on end. Henry thought he would never stop, and he was terrified that he would begin to weep before the interview was over, which would anger his father more than ever; he could feel his lip trembling and the tears gathering in his eyes. He was only saved by Mrs Gresham's rather timid knocking on the door.

'Frank, you do remember that the fly was ordered for half-past six, don't you?'

'The fly must wait until I have had this matter out with Henry.'

'Have you spoken to Julia about ... ?'

But at that moment Captain Gresham broke a finger

nail in his efforts to put in the last stud and gave a loud and irritable mutter which seemed to stop Mrs Gresham from saying more. 'So much for you, Henry, and I hope I have made it clear to you that you have got to take yourself in hand. As for you, Julia, what's this story that Miss Moule tells your mother about seeing you running around with those children from next door? I don't know who they are, or whether they are at all suitable for you to play with, and a lady can't be too careful about the people she associates with. You'd better play in your own garden in future.'

And that was all. Julia felt almost disappointed.

'He didn't seem to know anything about what you had done,' said Henry later, when the fly had collected his parents, and he had managed to get rid of the tears that choked his voice. 'Do you think the Old Dame didn't tell Mamma, or Mamma didn't tell Papa? Oh dear, I do hope he isn't going to find out later and start rowing all over again. Perhaps Mamma will talk to him in the fly about it.'

'Oh stop croaking,' Julia said irritably. 'You're always complaining about something.'

'Anyway, Mamma won't say anything.' Amy took her face out of the mug of milk that she was drinking as part of her supper. 'She'll be much too afraid of making Papa angry again. Did Papa say we weren't to play with the Holts again?'

'He just said we'd better play in our own garden in future. He didn't say anything about the Holts.'

'But it means we can't,' said Henry dismally. 'What are we going to say if they ask us to come in?'

But he need not have worried. The Holts made no attempt to ask them to play. Nor did Captain Gresham make any more reference to Julia's escapade. It was true that Mrs Gresham did speak to Julia about 'saying no more about it now, as Papa has already dealt with you. But I was very, very shocked at what Miss Moule told me, Julia. I could hardly believe that it was my daughter that she was referring to. Let there never be any repetition of anything like that.' But Mrs Gresham was so much less terrifying than the Captain that none of them worried much about her scoldings, unless they thought she was going to tell their father. Only Henry brooded about it in his gloomier moments. Surely his father could not have heard the full story, otherwise his anger would have been terrible indeed. Was there a fearful thunderbolt of wrath stored up somewhere, waiting for Julia?

But soon after, the school term started, and drove the episode even out of Henry's mind. This year, late summer turned into winter with hardly any autumn. After the end of the holidays they did not play in the garden again, for it rained heavily all through the rest of September, and for most of October. The leaves fell from the trees, and lay in a brown slush, clogging the gutters and making the pavements dangerously slippery. There was no question this year of swishing through the leaves as they lay in drifts at the side of the pavements, or of having surreptitious fights with armfuls of them.

They did not see the Holts at all, except as distant figures near the bottom of the road, heads down, walking against the rain. Wherever the Holts went for their walks, it was obviously not in the same direction as the Greshams, nor could their schools be near. Amy discovered from Mabel, who had it from Maud, the little maid at number 24, that Kate went to school at Antrim House, and she was very superior about this. Antrim House was reckoned by the girls of Holly Bank to be a poor sort of place with most inferior girls. Mabel had also heard that Richard did not go to school at all, he went out for lessons once or twice a week, but otherwise he stayed at home and worked there. Amy could quite often see his knees in the back room if she looked out of the bedroom window, but she got tired of doing this, and nobody seemed much interested in the information when she gave it. Besides, looking out of the bedroom window was a summer pastime, and this autumn was so cold.

Henry accepted with resignation the fact that the Holts now were forbidden to them. Richard he was afraid of, but he did like Kate, and she had been snatched away before there had been a chance to get to know her. She played just the pretend games that he had always wanted to play, only there was nobody among the Greshams who liked that sort of thing. He also regretted the apple tree. He was more than ever certain that he could climb it, given peace and time, and nobody watching him and telling him that he was a coward.

As for Julia, she had no intention of giving up the Holts. She was always hoping to see Richard in the street. She had never known anybody so clever as Richard. She felt she was set apart from everybody at school just from having known him, and when things went badly, if she was sharply rebuked for the untidiness of her work and her bad handwriting and if she was left out of other girls' confidences and laughed at because of her clumsiness, she would remember the glory of that journey to Westminster Abbey, and how she had defied all the things that these stupid people thought were proper. She was, she told herself, marked out for different things, and it did not matter if they laughed at her, because great people always had to face difficulties in their early years.

Towards the end of October a period of calm, bright weather set in. It was sunny and still, with pale blue skies, and the advance of winter seemed held up a little. The apple tree was now stripped of nearly all its leaves. A poor remnant clung to the branches, floating down at the faintest whisper of wind. One day, right at the end of October, Henry stood in the garden staring at the tree. It was a half-holiday at Mr Edgar's school, because they were half-way through the term, but Henry could not think what to do with it. Holly Bank had no holiday, so Julia was not available, and though Amy was at home recovering from a cold, she was useless as a companion. It was such a fine day, he felt he ought to be taking advantage of it, but there seemed nothing to do, and the precious time was rushing away and tomorrow he would be back at school. The garden seemed more than ever useless as a place to play. There wasn't a plant left in it now, the golden rod had been cut down to the ground and burnt on the bonfire; the bed in the middle of the grass had been emptied of all its plants and the bare earth waited for next year's geraniums and lobelias. Henry stood and looked up at the apple tree. Amy was beside him; the doll's house had been thoroughly turned out and polished and rearranged, and she was feeling bored and cross.

'Why are you standing and staring?' she demanded.

'I'd like to see the last leaf come down. It can't take long now.'

Amy was scornful. 'How silly. Why ever do you want to do that?'

'There you are. Nosey Parkering again,' remarked a voice from the other side of the hedge.

'That's Kate,' said Amy. She did not seem to mind about being called names; in any case, she was very glad to have some sort of distraction. 'Shall we come in?'

'Henry can, if he likes.'

Henry shook Amy's arm. 'We *can't*,' he whispered violently in her ear, as low as he could.

'Don't do that, it tickles,' Amy said loudly. 'Anyway, I can't hear what you're saying. Kate, we'll come in a minute. I'll just go and tell Mabel. Mamma's out.'

'I'm Catherine Mary Jocelyn to *you*,' said the voice coldly.

Amy did not give Henry time to remonstrate. She dashed in through the garden door shouting for Mabel. When Henry caught her up she was already in the kitchen talking urgently to her. Mabel, bare-armed and wearing house-maid's gloves, was cleaning the brass, which lay strewn over the table, cloudy with metal polish.

'I suppose you can go if your ma hasn't said not,' said Mabel, rubbing away at a brass shovel. 'Anyway, you'd be out of my way and that'd be a mercy. Go on, be off with you.'

Amy triumphantly banged the kitchen door shut and rushed towards the front door.

'Amy, we can't go,' said Henry, seizing her.

'Nobody said not.'

'You know Papa meant us not to.'

'That was ages ago. And anyway he didn't tell me and you needn't come if you don't want to.'

Henry did follow her, however. Nobody had actually said that they must not play with the Holts, Captain Gresham had just said that they ought to play in their own garden, and as Amy had said, that was ages ago. He might have changed his mind by now. They found Kate in the back garden, sitting sideways on a trestle made of a plank propped on two boxes, with her feet in two loops of rope. Tied to one end of the trestle was the stick with the stuffed sock, which Richard had told them was Kate's Arab stallion, and below, on the brick path, was the battered toy dog.

'Why, you've got Monarch there,' said Henry diffidently. He was not sure whether Kate allowed him to take part in her games. But Kate looked pleased.

'Yes, I am riding Sultan down Rotten Row, and

Monarch always follows us.' But then Kate caught sight of Amy, and she frowned heavily.

'Who said you could come in? I said Henry could, not you.'

Amy took no notice whatever. She was used to people trying to shake her off. She looked at the trestle and the stuffed sock with curiosity. 'Are you pretending to ride, or something?'

'Never you mind, Nosey Parker. You'd better find something to do with yourself. Henry and I are going to play. Only just be quiet, Richard's working.'

'I want to climb the tree like I did before,' said Amy calmly. 'Are there still some boxes in the shed?' She went over to the shed and peered in. 'You'll have to help me, Henry, they're heavy.'

Henry dragged them for her to the fence, and piled them one on top of each other. 'I'll test it to see that it's steady,' he called. He climbed rapidly on to the fence, and stood there, surveying the tree. He felt on fire to climb it, he was sure there could be no difficulty this time. 'Would you mind if I climbed it a little way,' he said to Kate. 'Then I'll come down and we'll play.'

'Go on. I'm sure you can climb better than your horrid little sister,' Kate said indifferently.

Henry did not hesitate this time. He swarmed up the tree, finding by instinct the best footholds, and striding upwards from branch to branch with an ease that he found intoxicating. The bare branches, the blue sky, the feeling of it being a holiday, even the smell of bonfire smoke from some nearby garden, all combined to make him feel dizzy with excitement, and he wanted to climb and climb and shout with all his lungs. Amy was outclassed this time. She stood on a branch near the bottom and swayed herself up and down, chanting 'I'm on my see-saw, I'm on my see-saw.' To which Henry, many feet above her head, answered with 'A life on the ocean wave.' He only knew the first line so he went on repeating it, rocking the branch he was holding with great violence.

The garden door opened. 'Hullo,' said Richard, 'you are making a row, aren't you.'

'There,' Kate said indignantly. 'You've gone and disturbed him. I told them you were working,' she complained.

Henry stopped his singing and peered anxiously down. Richard looked more spindly than ever, and his hair was standing on end as though he had been rubbing his fingers through it. 'I'm sorry. We won't make any more noise, I promise.'

Richard ignored the apology. 'Where's your sister?'

'She's down there.' Henry pointed in the direction of Amy.

'I don't mean that one, she's hardly worth considering. I mean your big sister, the one that's going to be great.'

Henry laughed uneasily. 'Oh she's at school, she hasn't got a half-holiday like me. Amy's only here because she's had a cold.'

'So it's a half-holiday that gives rise to all these high spirits. It's had the same effect on Woggle too. Hasn't even a brisk canter down the Row on Sultan been any good, Woggle mine?' Richard strolled over to the plank and the two boxes and scrutinized them closely. 'Dear me, Sultan seems to be rather lame in the off foreleg. What do you say?'

Kate joined him. 'Yes, I think you're right. I'll tell the head groom to attend to it at once.'

Richard went back to the tree. 'Well, Henry, you've performed the task I set very satisfactorily. You can come down from the tree when you're ready.'

Henry did not really want to come down, but he obeyed at once. After all, it was the Holts' tree, and it was extraordinarily nice of Richard to make no reference to that fiasco at the end of the summer holidays, and to behave as though the task had been performed as soon as it was set. He swung down on to the fence, felt for the boxes, and jumped to the ground.

'Very nice,' Richard said thoughtfully. 'Well, you have all accomplished your tasks now, and have gone through a period of probation. I think we can initiate you into the society.'

'Kate hasn't done any task,' Amy pointed out.

'Woggle is exempt. She is a Holt.'

'It's not fair,' flashed Amy. Injustice roused her more than anything else. 'Why should we all do these horrible things and you not? You even made me throw away my rabbit.' She pointed angrily to the chimney where Mrs Vonnister had disappeared.

Kate flew to the defence of her brother. 'Don't you start telling Richard what's fair and what isn't. Who do you think you are, I'd like to know?'

Richard lifted his hand. 'Steady, Woggle, steady. Who are we to be troubled by this little insect's buzzing?' He turned his back on Amy and spoke to Henry. 'Tonight then expect your initiation into the SAGBOHEICIM. At half-past five in this house.'

'We'll have to be back at six,' Henry faltered. 'Because that's when Mamma comes in. Today's Tuesday, and it's her day for calling,' he explained uneasily.

'By six o'clock you will be members of the SAGBO-HEICIM,' Richard assured him. Then he swung round suddenly to Amy. 'You can set your mind at rest. What-ever has been the fate of your rabbit, it is no longer at the top of that chimney.'

'That's right.' Kate stared up. 'The lead's gone. It used to dangle down the chimney pot. Monarch's best red lead. It was much better than any dirty old rabbit of yours, Miss Amy.'

But Amy could not be appeased. She muttered all the afternoon about the unfairness of the Holts not having to do any tests, and complained to Julia when she came home from school. Julia paid no attention, she was far too excited at the prospect of initiation into the Society, and concerned with rushing through her homework before half-past five. Still muttering, Amy came with Henry and Julia when they set off for the next door house. It was a clear, cold evening, already nearly dark.

'I asked Ellen if she could come and call for us just before six,' Henry confided to Julia. 'Then we can be quite sure we'll be home before Mamma comes in.'

Kate rushed to the front door to open it for them. She seemed to be in a wild state of excitement. 'We're to go to the back room, then to the cellar,' she said breathlessly. 'Richard's working out something wonderful. He's been preparing it since teatime. And it's awfully good of him to play with us at all when he's got such a lot of work to do,' she added aggressively.

But Richard was reading when they went in; none of them had ever seen him without a book in his hand. On the table was a collection of objects which seemed to be meant for the initiation ceremony, though it was difficult to tell in the Holts' house just what was put down for a special purpose, and what had been abandoned there and forgotten. There were tea things that looked as though they had been left for a day or more, books and bits of paper, as usual, but there were also some candles stuck into egg-cups and bottles, a pile of old curtains, and a large paper knife.

'Before you aspiring SAGBO's can be initiated you will have to be sacrificed,' announced Richard, putting down his book at last. 'You had better each choose a candle, and mind you look after it because if your candle goes out you'll just have to endure the darkness. And these are your robes. Go on, put them on.' He pointed to the curtains.

Julia felt a rush of excitement. This was the sort of game that it needed Richard to invent. None of them could have possibly done it. Eagerly she took the top curtain and put it on. It was a rusty brown plush with several tears in it, and was enormously long with huge wooden rings sewn into the top. She wound the folds round her as best she could. Amy stared.

'Why have we got to wear curtains? Julia does look funny in hers with the rings hanging down. Can I have one without tears?'

'How this wearisome little insect does buzz,' remarked Richard. 'Now then, is everybody ready? Let us proceed to the candle lighting ceremony, then.'

He picked up a box of matches from the table and a candle stuck into the top of a bottle labelled 'Dr Isaac's Hair Restorer'. 'Aunt B bought it for Father. But Father of course would have nothing to do with it. I tipped away most of the stuff but there's still a bit left. We might try it on Monarch, Woggle, when he gets mange.'

Kate was outraged. 'Monarch doesn't get mange. He's much too well-bred.'

'All right, keep your hair on. (That wasn't meant to be a joke but you can laugh if you want to.) Now then my SAGBO's, light your candles at this flame.' He seemed to be in a very good mood as he held his lighted candle out in front of him. 'Kneel to receive your light.'

They all knelt down, even Amy, and lighted their candles from Richard's. Solemnly he moved the bottle of Dr Isaac's Hair Restorer round the half-circle of kneeling figures until everybody held a light. Then, brandishing it above his head he moved to the door. They followed, clutching their curtains. The candles, which had not been very noticeable in the gaslight, seemed to grow brighter and larger flames in the dimness of the passage. From a distant room they could hear the whirring of a sewing machine and Aunt B's voice singing raucously 'My old man, he said follow the van and don't dilly dally on the way.'

'This way,' said Richard, turning abruptly. Their candles flickered as they swung round the corner, down a short passage which led to a back door. Half-way down it, he stopped and fumbled with the bolt on a door under the stairs.

'Mind your robes as we go down the stairs. We don't want any of them torn.'

'Mine is torn already,' remarked Amy. 'But I didn't do it.'

Stone steps led down to the cellar, and a smell of damp and of coal came up from it, and chilly air, which made them all shiver. Henry, at the back, looked longingly at the light which he was leaving. Aunt B was making such a cheerful noise, he wished he could go into her sewing room and sit with her. He followed the line of small flickering flames down in the depths of the cellar. They all stood at the bottom of the steps, clustering round Richard, able to see only each other's faces.

'There are a good many packing cases and unwanted pieces of furniture down here,' remarked Richard, 'so take care of your shins and tread in my footsteps. We are making for the far end of the cellar.' He turned, and his light went with him. That left the four of them standing in the darkness which seemed completely black; they had not been down there long enough to get used to it.

'I'm coming,' shouted Amy, and turned and hurried after him. Kate and Julia followed. Henry peered back at the rectangle of light at the top of the steps, which he was being made to leave for the black unknown. Shivering, he went after the others, but he had not gone a step or two before he tripped and fell over a box. He saved himself from sprawling headlong, but his candle and its holder crashed to the ground with a splintering of glass and went out. Now he was left in total darkness. Ahead of him the candles of the others threw fantastic shapes on the walls.

'My candle's gone out,' he shouted in a quavering voice.

'You owe Aunt B a penny on the bottle,' Richard called back from what seemed a long way off. 'If you broke that too.'

His voice sounded as though he was speaking from a tomb. The others laughed, miles and miles away. In a wild panic, Henry started off after them. But it is as difficult to run through total darkness as it is to run through deep water. He lurched from side to side, barking his shins on boxes and packing cases, fumbling at the cold, damp walls, thinking of hands that might be stretched out to grab at him, to put their fingers round his throat. It was only a few yards down the passage, but it seemed half a mile before he saw candle-light and the others standing in a group inside a door. They turned to look at him.

'Enter Henry, blood-stained and wild-eyed,' remarked Richard. 'You seem to have wounded yourself on the way. Or is it only dirt?'

'Blood *and* dirt,' said Amy, peering.

'Let it pass. I will now explain the nature of the rites we are about to perform. In the middle of the room you see a slab. This is the altar slab. On it the hapless victim will be tied—and that is each of you dear, good people in turn. I am the arch-SAGBO and sacrificer, and while we chant the sacrificial hymn the victim of the moment will be disembowelled—by me, with this knife.'

'Does disembowel mean cut him up? Are you really

going to?' asked Amy with deep interest.

'And wouldn't you just love it if he was,' said Kate disgustedly. 'Who's going to be the first victim, Richard?'

'That is just what I am going to decide now, Woggle mine. Now, stand in line all of you.'

They shuffled into a line, giggling and fidgeting nervously. Richard hitched his robes round his shoulders and held his candle high, and then he made jabs at them with his paper-knife, intoning: 'Ah, ra, chickera, roly, poly, pickena, kinny, minny, festi, shanti-poo, ickerman chickerman, chinee-choo.' At the word 'chinee-choo' the paper knife stopped and pointed at Amy. 'Here is our victim, an unworthy one I fear, but let it pass. Lead her to the altar and rope her down. Advance, maiden, and do not resist.'

Kate and Richard led Amy to the huge stone table which took up most of the middle of the floor. Presumably it was meant to store food on, but now it had been swept clear of everything except a piece of rope.

'Lay thyself upon the holy place and turn thy mind to higher things.' Richard spoke in a deep sepulchral voice that made Henry shiver, but Amy was quite undaunted.

'Do you mean I've got to lie down here? I hope it's clean, things in cellars aren't, usually. I haven't got to put my head down, have I? It'll get all cobwebby.' Amy gave a little squeal as Richard pressed her down on the stone. 'Ooh, it is cold and hard.'

Richard began roping her to the slab. 'Prepare thyself for they holy doom,' he said in the same unnatural voice. 'When the first ray of light touches thy heart then shall this knife pierce thy entrails.' He held the knife above his head and it gleamed for a moment in the light of the candle that Kate held. 'SAGBO Kate, let the light that you hold travel up the victim from her feet until it reaches her heart. Then will I strike.' He retreated into the shadows round the edge of the cellar. Henry could

not see him properly, only the light from his candle.

'Let all lights be extinguished except that held by SAGBO Kate,' commanded Richard. His own went out, and then Julia's and now there was nothing but a mass of black shadows, and a tiny glimmer from the middle of the room where Kate was shielding her candle with her hand. From the corner where Richard had been standing there suddenly came a loud and mournful chanting:

'Dost thou see it coming?
Victim, turn thy eye.
Now the SAGBO *forces*
Close in secretly.'

Richard's voice was very unmelodious, but Henry recognized the tune he was singing. It was surely taken from a Lent hymn, all about the hordes of Satan prowling around, a hymn which even with Christian words never failed to make him shudder. He had only to remember the tune when he was lying in bed, to feel that the dark was full of horrible grinning devils. Now it made him sick with fright. He closed his eyes and clenched his nails into the palm of his hand. There was a swishing over the floor near him, much giggling from Amy and squeals that Richard was tickling her, and then everything seemed to be over.

'The first member of the SAGBOHEICIM stands initiated,' said Richard. 'The first and the unworthiest. Let her stand apart while we select a second.' Richard intoned the same rhyme, and the knife fell on Julia. Again the hymn was chanted, the light moved over the slab, there was a gasp from Julia, and she was allowed to climb down, initiated. The counting-out rhyme was said over Kate and Henry, and it fell to Kate to be the third initiated member of the SAGBOHEICIM. Henry stood sweating in the darkness, pressing his hands over his ears to try to keep out the horrifying chant, but knowing as he did it that it was useless, because he must be sacrificed next and there was no escape. If only they forgot about him in the darkness, if only Ellen would come for them now.

But of course they did not forget him. He was led to the slab, he was too frightened to see by whom, and he felt the rope going over his legs and then up again on the other side, over his chest. He caught a glimpse of

Richard's face in the glimmer of the candle that somebody was holding; he was wearing the curtain over his
head like a monk's cowl. Perhaps it was the ghost of a
monk and not Richard at all. The figure moved back
and disappeared into the darkness, the dreadful, mournful dirge started, and voices from all round the cellar
joined in. The candle flame appeared above his feet. But
it never reached his heart, because by that time Henry
was screaming and screaming and struggling against the
ropes.

CHAPTER 8

Mrs Vonnister the Trouble-Maker

Through his screams Henry was faintly aware of hearing a doorbell. But he did not pay any attention, his mind was only on the terrible light advancing nearer him, and the figure in the monk's cowl, holding a poised knife and lurking somewhere in the shadows waiting to strike. He had his eyes squeezed shut, but this could not drive out the horrifying image. He did not notice that the sinister chanting had stopped and that there were other voices in the cellar, and when somebody started shaking him he only screamed louder than ever. Then a man's voice from somewhere beside him spoke angrily.

'Stop this mumbo jumbo at once, Richard, and give me a knife to cut the boy's rope. And for heaven's sake be quick or all the neighbours will be calling out the fire brigade.'

Henry opened his eyes then. He recognized that voice, it was Mr Holt, and the new fright that this produced was like a glass of cold water being thrown over him, it shocked him out of his hysterical terror of the monkish figure. There was silence in the cellar now, and from the top of the steps, a long way off, he heard Ellen's voice.

'What are you doing to him, you naughty children? Stop it at once, I say, or I'll get the Captain to you.' She sounded breathless and very agitated.

Then came Aunt B's voice. 'Tell me quick, is someone murdered? For mercy's sake, can't anybody answer?'

'It's all right, nobody's hurt as far as I can see,' Mr Holt shouted back. He cut the last bit of rope, and Henry, stiff and trembling, sat up and swung his legs over the edge of the slab. He felt very weak and ashamed.

Mr Holt, gripping him by the shoulder, and carrying a lamp in his other hand, propelled him through the cellar and up the steps. At the top, by the door, were clustered Ellen and Aunt B, together with Julia, Amy, Richard and Kate.

'Well, what's wrong with him?' demanded Ellen, seizing him and peering at him.

'Nothing that a strong dose of sal volatile won't put right,' said Mr Holt drily. 'These little fiends seem to have been doing their best to scare him out of his wits. Well, if I'm needed no longer I'll go back to my study. Cheer up, young man, the strongest nerves would have been shattered by my son's carryings on. Mine would have been, for a start.'

'You mean to say that all that noise fit to awake the dead was just because he was frightened?' demanded Ellen incredulously. 'Well, I've never heard the like.'

Aunt B fanned herself with a paper pattern that she was holding. She was red in the face, and her blue satin blouse was heaving alarmingly. 'I thought at the very least it was Jack the Ripper at work, such a cater-wauling and screeching, it made my blood run cold. I even heard it above the noise of the sewing machine, and that's not something that often happens.'

'And I heard it on the front doorstep,' said Ellen. 'It strikes me it was lucky I came when I did.'

'I wasn't frightened,' said Amy virtuously. 'I thought it was a very funny sort of game.'

'Just a game was it? Then you all ought to be ashamed of yourselves, that's all I can say.'

'I don't see why we should be ashamed,' said Amy truculently. 'It was a perfectly good game, we were being initiated. It was Henry who spoilt it all by being a baby and screaming. I didn't scream when they did the same things to me.'

'That child needs taking in hand,' remarked Richard

to nobody in particular.

'Well, you're not taking anybody else in hand in this house,' said Aunt B. 'Enough's enough, that's what I say, and I'm sure that's what young Henry would say too.' She smacked the shrinking Henry across the back in a jolly way.

'I'm sure it's very nice of you to take it this way, miss,' said Ellen. 'Screaming the place down like that, I'm downright ashamed of them. Now come along at once, all of you.'

She was very short with them on the way home; she had been frightened, and it had a bad effect on her temper. 'Carrying on like that and making such a scene, Master Henry, and you going to be a soldier. You ought to be showing those children next door how to behave instead of disgracing yourself in front of them and making me apologize for you to that person, I'm sure she's no lady. A person, that's all she is. I've a good mind to tell the Captain and all.'

'But you won't, will you?' said Julia aghast. They were standing in the kitchen now.

'You'll have to tell Papa that you said we could go in there,' remarked Amy.

'And I'm sure I don't mind doing that, Miss Amy,' said Ellen indignantly. 'I did what I thought was right and I'm not ashamed of it.'

They were all standing uncomfortably round the table, Ellen thoroughly cross, Amy defiant, Julia looking uneasily at Henry, who with drooping head was pleating the tablecloth between limp fingers. At that moment the front door bell rang. Ellen straightened her cap and smoothed down her apron.

'That's you ma I suppose, or your pa. What I'm going to say to them I just don't know.'

Uneasily they all clustered near the kitchen door to hear what she was going to say. You could never tell with Ellen, she was a chancy sort of person. Sometimes she might seem to be on your side, and just as you felt thoroughly confident that she was an ally, you would suddenly find that she was on the other side, of your parents. But it certainly was not their father or their mother that was in the hall.

'A filthy thing like that ours! Pardon me, but I think you must be mistaken, miss. No, neither the Captain nor the mistress are at home just now. I don't know when they'll be in, I'm sure.'

'I think it's the Old Dame in the hall,' announced Amy in a whisper. 'Perhaps she's come because she's going to complain about Henry screaming.'

Henry's heart gave a thud, it felt as though it was going to jump out of him. Then he remembered. 'What did Ellen mean about a filthy thing then?' he whispered back.

'Perhaps she's found Mrs Vonnister.' When Julia said this she had meant it as a joke, but in a flash it came over her that it was not so silly after all. The lead that had dangled down the chimney pot for weeks, marking Mrs Vonnister's presence, had disappeared. Perhaps the bundle had edged its way down the chimney and had suddenly fallen into the Old Dame's grate. She giggled as she thought about it. The others turned and stared and wanted to know what the joke was. Julia told them as well as she could for laughing, it sounded so ludicrous put into words. But Amy didn't take it so lightly. She clenched her hands.

'If that Old Dame has got Mrs Vonnister, she's just got to give her back, that's all. She's mine.'

'Sssh,' said Henry at the door. He was anxiously trying to hear what was being said in the hall. 'Oh goodness, now Mamma's come in.'

Ellen came back into the kitchen, and they clustered

round her. 'Was it the Old Dame, Ellen? What was wrong?'

'It was Miss Moule all right,' said Ellen grimly. 'Well, you are in it up to your necks and no mistake. However could you have gone and done such a thing, Miss Amy? Throwing that rabbit of yours into her chimney! You must have clean took leave of your senses. And I thought you were supposed to be so fond of it. You carried on alarming enough last time I gave it to Mrs Marsh to wash.'

'It wasn't me,' said Amy, bristling with indignation. But she got no further because Julia stamped heavily on her foot and she squealed.

'But how did the Old Dame know the rabbit came from us?' Julia asked hastily to cover the noise that Amy was making.

'That rabbit was wrapped up in the old bit of towel that Miss Amy calls her cuddler, and the towel had your ma's name on it, as large as life. My word, Miss Moule was that angry. She said her chimney was smoking fit to kill them all, just after it had been swept, too. So she sent for the sweep and he pushed out that old rabbit of yours. Well, your ma's in the drawing-room talking to her now, and I wouldn't be in your shoes when your pa gets to hear about it. Now run along to the school-room, all of you.'

As soon as they got to the schoolroom, Julia shut the door carefully and told the others with great urgency that whatever happened they were to keep the Holts out of this. Her voice became impassioned and eloquent as she pleaded with them. But it was not her passion that convinced Amy and Henry. Henry wanted no persuading to keep silence about the Holts. He had got it into his head that if the least whisper reached his father's ears about their friendship with Kate and Richard, he would thunder as he had never thundered before, and would forbid all connection with them immediately. As for Amy, Julia had offered her tuppence of next week's pocket money and her best lace-trimmed handkerchief as a doll's counterpane. She had also said that she, Julia, would take the blame for having thrown Mrs Vonnister. Henry stirred himself at this.

'No, it'll have to be me,' he said gloomily. 'You're a girl. Papa will know you couldn't possibly have thrown it. Do you think we'll all have to go up to his dressing-room?'

They crouched in front of the schoolroom fire, waiting for him to come in. Their mother had merely said, with pursed lips and a severe expression, 'Of course, I shall have to tell Papa. Miss Moule is very angry indeed, and I am sure I would be in the circumstances.' They shivered; the fire had sunk very low. Ellen had not made it up since teatime, and refused to get more coal now, when, as she said, the room wouldn't be needed after the Captain came in. Henry reflected sadly that it was rather hard that staying up late, a treat in most families, should be kept among the Greshams for when someone was specially angry with them. And would Ellen tell his parents about the terrible episode in the Holts' cellar? It had momentarily been driven out of his mind by the Old Dame, but now it came back again, his terror, shame, and humiliation, and he stared at the grey embers of the fire, pressing himself against the fireguard for warmth, sick at the memory of his disgrace and at the thought of what his father would say if he was told.

But when Captain Gresham did come in he was surprisingly mild. It was a ridiculous escapade, he said looking at the shrinking Henry, who, though weak in the knees with fright, tried to keep his eyes steady, for there was nothing his father detested so much as people not looking him straight in the eye. Whatever could have induced Henry to go bombarding old ladies' chimneys? Well, there was to be no repetition of this sort of thing, and Henry would have to write a note apologizing for his behaviour.

Henry could hardly believe that they had escaped so lightly. 'I just don't see,' he said over and over again. 'It was much worse than me not climbing the Holts' tree and that was the worst row I have ever had, almost. Why, he didn't even send for us to his dressing-room, or say we weren't to have cake for tea.'

'That's because he thinks that throwing things is what boys who are going to be soldiers ought to do,' said Amy loftily. 'None of you understand Papa. I do.'

But Amy was not so superior and grownup the next day by any means. In fact, Julia and Henry had not seen her in such a tantrum since she was quite a small girl. She went into the kitchen, meaning to ask Ellen to give Mrs Vonnister to Mrs Marsh to wash next Monday. By some lucky chance Mrs Vonnister had come back and Amy thought that it would be ridiculous not to make use of her. But there was Ellen with a flushed face and the top lifted off the stove just about to poke Mrs Vonnister inside.

'How dare you,' Amy screamed. 'Stop it at once. Give her back to me, I say.'

Ellen straightened herself in her surprise, and stood with the poker in one hand and Mrs Vonnister in her sooty shroud in the other. The red lead, black now, trailed down on the ground.

'Well, of all the naughty ways to talk, Miss Amy. If your ma could hear you now what would she say? No, I've had my orders and that nasty rabbit of yours has got to be burnt. And burnt it should have been long ago—eight years old and still taking a toy to bed!' She pushed the dirty bundle into the stove, poked in the

lead after it, and slammed down the top of the stove.
Amy gave a howl of fury and flung herself on Ellen,
pushing her violently out of the way while she pulled
the top off the stove and peered in. But flames were
already consuming Mrs Vonnister and roaring up the
chimney. Amy flung down the iron plate which closed
the stove, so that it crashed among the fire irons in the
hearth with a hideous clatter, and started screaming
and weeping and pummelling Ellen. The noise brought
Henry and Julia, who had been getting ready for school,
racing downstairs. They came into the kitchen just as
Amy, beside herself with fury, was shrieking: 'It wasn't
me who threw her, I didn't want her to go. It was those
horrible, horrible . . .' But at this point Julia managed
to drag her off while Henry, who was a favourite with
the maids, stayed behind to try to soothe Ellen and
persuade her not to tell their mother.

With difficulty Julia pulled Amy into the schoolroom.
Amy was shaking with angry sobs, her breath was
coming in gasps, she could not have stopped crying if
she wanted to, and there were only five minutes left
before they would have to leave for school with Mabel.
'That horrible, horrible, Richard,' she said with a violent
gasp for breath between each word. 'He threw her there,
and now Ellen's gone and burnt her. And he won't make
Kate do anything, not anything. I'm going to get that
dog of hers and burn it and see how she likes that. And
I'm going to tell Papa about them.'

It was only by promising Amy the whole of next
Saturday's pocket money, Henry's as well as her own,
that Julia managed to ward off that danger. (She also
said that Amy could have another lace-edged handkerchief, and reminded her how much her best doll's bed
needed it.) When Mabel came to find them, Amy was
still tearful and very swollen about the eyes, but at least
she wasn't crying loudly, and by the time they went

in to their mother to say goodbye it was too late for anybody to make many enquiries as to what had upset Amy.

All the way to school they lagged behind Mabel, Amy sullen and dragging her feet while Julia tried to reason with her, pointing out that Mrs Vonnister had departed long ago and Amy had not minded then, she had even enjoyed it. Why the fuss now that she had come back? But Amy refused to be reasoned with. She just said that she hated Richard, she hated Kate, she thought their old society was stupid—she wasn't going to have her horizons broadened or whatever silly thing they wanted to do. And anyway it was all unfair, why didn't Kate have to do a task? Why had Mrs Vonnister got to go and not Kate's dog? She kept on and on repeating how unfair it was the whole of the way to school. Julia felt exhausted by argument, and quite limp at the thought of the morning's lessons ahead of her.

Julia did not see Amy for the rest of the day, but she looked at her anxiously at four o'clock when she went to fetch her from the junior cloakroom. It was clear that Amy was in one of her bad moods, she was tight-lipped and silent. She marched beside Mabel and would not say a word. Suddenly she stood still. Mabel, who had gone on a few steps, looked back.

'Oh come along, Miss Amy, do. It's too cold to stand around.'

But Amy was staring at something in the distance on the other side of the road. 'I can see Kate,' she said loudly. 'I'm just going to tell her what I think of her and her horrible brother and that horrible society.' She had rushed across the street and was pounding down the pavement on the other side before either Julia or Mabel could come to their senses.

They hurried after her, of course, but by the time they caught her up Amy was well into her stride. She was standing there, talking loudly, her face flushed red with anger, while Kate scowled, her shoulders hunched, her hands thrust deep into her pockets.

'And you can tell Richard what I say about your society,' Amy was saying shrilly as Julia reached her.

Kate shrugged. 'As if Richard would care what you thought. He's far too clever for any of you, that's the trouble.'

Amy was lashed into greater fury by this indifference of Kate's. 'And you can tell him that it's about time you and he did some tasks instead of always making us. He took my rabbit away from me, didn't he. Well, if he doesn't take your stupid dog, Monarch, or whatever he's called, next time I'm going to, so there.'

'That was to do you good, to broaden your horizons, though not much good it seems to have done you,' said Kate coldly. And *I* let you have Monarch's red lead, remember that.'

'It's been burnt then,' said Amy triumphantly. 'The Old Dame brought it back and Mrs Vonnister too, and Ellen burnt them both, I saw her.'

At last she had managed to rouse Kate. 'You let them burn that red lead that Richard bought me!' She clenched her hands and looked as though she was going to hit Amy. 'You nasty horrible little beast. I wish we'd never bothered with any of you. I hope we won't see you again, none of you, never.' She pushed pell mell down the street while Amy stared triumphantly after her.

'She's crying, and she's got a hole in her stocking, look. Well, we won't have to play with *them* any more.'

CHAPTER 9

Aunt B Tries

For three months on end they did not see the Holts. November, December, January went past without a sign of them. Whereas before Julia and Henry had lingered in the road, on their way back from school, on their walks, hoping that they might see Richard or Kate, now they hurried, with their heads down. After what Amy had said to Kate, it would be very embarrassing to meet the Holts. Julia had decided that she would try to apologize, but very likely they would refuse to listen to her.

But in any case it was winter, and nobody could have wanted to linger in the roads. Before Christmas sleety rains had lashed down, whipped by north-east winds. There never seemed to be a day when the Greshams did not come in from school wet. After Christmas icy weather came, black frost and fog at the same time, and it was misery to have to set foot outside. The only sign that there was anybody living at the Holts' house at all was the smoke from their chimney and a glimmer of light from the room that Aunt B used as her sewing room.

Then, one Saturday morning, the last Saturday in January, when Julia was standing in the road waiting for Henry and Amy, she saw Kate. They were all going to spend their pocket money at Portway's, but the other two had decided that it was even colder than usual and had rushed back indoors to get their mufflers. Julia was stamping her feet and banging her hands together when out of the fog which hid most of the road, Kate appeared. Her hands were deep in her pockets, her head was sunk forward, her shoulders hunched, and she looked thoroughly depressed. Julia, short-sighted as she was, could tell this by the way Kate was walking.

'Hullo,' said Julia at last, as Kate, still with her eyes on the ground, turned to go into her house. She walked down the road a few steps towards her.

Kate paused with her hand on the gate and looked up for the first time. Her face was mauve from the cold, her hair damp and lank, and the fog had clung to her coat and even to her eyebrows in tiny little beads of wet. But she brightened a little when she saw Julia. 'Oh hullo.'

Then there was an awkward silence. Both of them remembered what had happened on the last occasion they had met. Julia wondered uneasily whether Kate was still brooding over Monarch's lead and the things that Amy had said to her. Furtively she looked back at the house, to see whether Amy was on her way out yet.

'How's Richard?' she ventured. (She had to say something.)

Kate's expression became despondent again. 'I don't see him much these days.'

Julia was astonished. 'Has he gone to Christ's already then?'

'No, of course he hasn't. Everything would be all right if he had. I don't know who invented scholarships, but whoever it was ought to be tortured,' Kate said violently. 'It's making him so miserable, you can't think. He just works all the time without stopping—never goes out or anything except when he has to go to lessons with Mr James. He won't even let me stay in the same room with him, he sends me out all the time.'

'What do you do then?' said Julia aghast.

Kate shrugged. 'Just sit on the stairs. It's so cold, though. Sometimes I wrap the ironing blanket round me. And sometimes I go and sit with Aunt B, if she's not too busy. Or with Maud, the kitchen's warm enough.

Only Maud talks so (and she does sniff, that's worse), and Aunt B says she doesn't get on with her work if I'm there, so if she finds me in the kitchen she usually sends me out.' She hesitated and looked at Julia rather diffidently. 'I suppose I couldn't come and play in your house sometimes?' Then she glared at the ground in her embarrassment.

Julia was appalled; she did not know what to say. Of course, it was quite out of the question. She and Henry had been doing all they could to keep the Holts from their parents, how could they possibly invite Kate in? It would mean asking their mother, who in turn would refer it to their father. It just could not be done. 'I don't know,' she said uneasily. 'It's a bit difficult. I mean, Mamma would have to ask your aunt. And we don't have people in to play, not often that is . . .' She did not know how long she could have kept up these rambling excuses, but luckily, before she had to think up any more, Amy came rushing out of the house followed by Henry. To cover her embarrassment she talked to them loudly.

'Richard's working very hard for his scholarship. Sometimes he doesn't even let Kate in the same room.'

'He's very unkind then,' said Amy. 'I wouldn't let Julia send me out of the room. Not for anything.'

'How dare you say he's unkind?' flashed Kate. 'What do you know about it, anyway? It's because he's working and nobody in your family knows anything about work. Richard's a genius, he's different from anybody else—especially from little idiots like you.' Kate stuck out her tongue at Amy and rushed off. They heard the gate slam behind her and feet running up the path.

'Do you know,' Amy announced, 'she's crying again. She does seem to cry a lot.'

Julia felt ill at ease. 'Come on if you're ready, we'll go to Portway's,' she said unnecessarily loudly.

But all the way there she turned her clumsy excuses to Kate over in her mind. Finally she confided in Henry hoping that he would support her. 'I mean, we couldn't possibly ask her in, could we? Not without Mamma knowing that we know her and asking all sorts of questions and then saying Kate and Richard weren't suitable.'

But Henry was unhelpful. 'I don't know,' he said vaguely. Then he added wistfully, 'It is funny, Kate wanting to come to our house. I would much rather go to hers.'

Julia was astonished. 'Why? Do you want to look at the books and things? You couldn't climb the tree in this weather.'

'I don't know. Nobody ever seems to get angry or mind what you do. Aunt B's so nice, sometimes I think she would be rather nice to have as a mother.' He stopped at once, horrified at what he had said.

'If *I* wanted Kate to come in and play I would ask Papa,' Amy announced. 'But I don't. Look, here's Portway's. What are you going to buy, Henry?'

They were still standing outside Portway's some five minutes later, staring into the windows and discussing what they were going to have. Amy wanted two sugar mice, a pink and a white one. But she also wanted a sherbet fountain, and could not decide whether to give up the pink or the white mouse. They were so engrossed in the window that they did not hear anybody coming up, and jumped violently when Aunt B's voice rang out from behind them.

'Well, if it isn't the kiddies from next door. Why, you are strangers these days. And where have you been hiding yourselves? Nowhere our Kay could find you, I know that. I tell you what, why don't you come to tea with her and Richard and cheer them up a bit? There's Richard working himself into a decline and poor little

Kay moping round the place, they need taking out of themselves, that's a fact. Look, you come to tea today and give them a treat for once. I'll tell them I've got a nice little surprise for them, and we'll have some chocolate eclairs and some meringues to celebrate.'

There was nothing they could say except thank Aunt B and say they would ask their mother if they might. But Julia wondered just how nice Richard and Kate would think the surprise was. Perhaps Mrs Gresham would say they could not go; this was the only glimmer of hope. And when they came into the drawing-room and found their father was there both Julia and Henry felt sure there would be a fuss. But Mrs Gresham made no difficulties, she just said she thought it was a little odd that Miss Holt had not called to give the invitation. Then she turned to Captain Gresham.

'I suppose you have no objection, Frank?'

'Objection to what? The children going out to tea? Certainly not. The schoolroom has been a bedlam the last few Saturday afternoons. I shall be thankful for a little peace.'

'I don't suppose he knows who we're going out to tea with,' Amy remarked sagely later on. 'Papa doesn't listen to half the things Mamma tells him, and I'm sure he would have paid much more attention if he had known we were going next door. He's always talking about seeing Mr Holt and how untidy he looks. Do you think they will have a tea like the other one? Cream cakes and all those sort of things?' Amy had forgotten her rage with the Holts. Besides, she was bored with winter Saturday afternoons that kept them in the schoolroom. Henry was pleased at the prospect of going next door, even though he was nervous of Richard's cleverness. Only Julia dreaded it, wondering how she would ever be able to face Kate again.

At four o'clock the Greshams presented themselves on

the doorstep of number 24. The fog was even thicker and it had become very dark. The gas lamp further up the road had already been lit and shone feebly through the thick white mist. Amy said she was sure it was people's breath, and that it wouldn't be anything like so bad in the country where there weren't many people, as in the town where there were hundreds and hundreds of them walking round the streets breathing out mist. Julia listened not to Amy but for sounds inside the Holts' house. Presently Maud pulled the door open. She looked a little neater than usual because she had changed into her afternoon uniform, but her cap was crooked, her hair was a haystack and she had a smut on her forehead.

'You'd better keep your coats on,' she said, staring at them and sniffing. 'It's enough to freeze your blood in the dining-room. I'm just going to take in the tea now.' She went off down the passage to the kitchen and left them standing there. Presently the door of the sewing room opened and Aunt B put her head out. She was wearing a moleskin cape and had a feather boa twisted round her neck.

'Has Maud gone and left you here all this time? What a fool that girl is. Excuse the costume, but I'm trying to keep myself from turning into an iceberg. Come along into the dining-room; it's perishing cold, I'm afraid, but you can't keep fires burning in every single room in the house. Where are those children? Katie, Richie!' she called down the passage.

The door of the backroom opened at the bottom of the passage, and Richard appeared. Kate came shambling up behind him, with a sulky mouth and her eyes fixed on the ground. 'Here are your little friends standing and freezing all by themselves,' said Aunt B loudly, 'and nobody looking after them. Well, come along into the dining-room now. Maud will be bringing

the teapot through in a minute. Katie, go and knock on
your Daddy's door and tell him tea's ready.'

Still wearing their coats, the Greshams went into the
dining-room. It was certainly very cold there and very
gloomy, with the stained brown wallpaper and dark
brown paint, and newspapers and books were strewn
everywhere. The table had rather a dirty cloth on and
was laid with a lavish tea, buttered buns, rich fruit
cake, jam tarts, and all sorts of cream-filled pastries.
Aunt B looked at it with satisfaction.

'Nice to have a spready tea for once,' she remarked.
'Helps to keep the cold out, food does, I always say.'

Mr Holt came in, his hair in untidy wisps, his feet
pushed into down-at-heel brown carpet slippers. He
smiled vaguely at the Greshams and cast an eye over the
tea-table.

'Somebody's birthday?' he said.

'Just a little surprise to cheer up the kiddies,' said
Aunt B brightly. 'They've had a bad time of it lately
what with Richard working so hard and it being so cold.
And all work and no play makes Dick a dull boy, that's
what I say.' She beamed round the table, but only the
Greshams smiled politely back.

The Holt children did not seem to be enjoying their
surprise very much; the Greshams stole glances at them
from time to time. Kate, gobbling down tarts and buns,
never lifted her eyes from her plate except to thrust her
cup at Aunt B to be filled up. Richard, on the other
hand, hardly ate anything; he nibbled all round a jam
tart in mouse-like bites and stared straight in front of
him. There was very little talking. Aunt B with her
usual air of cheerfulness rattled out questions which
the Greshams did their best to answer. Amy, as the
meal progressed, rattled on as cheerfully as Aunt B
herself, and talked about their Christmas party, about
the concert their school was giving, and the skirt dance

she was learning at dancing class.

At last tea came to an end. Julia and Henry were sorry. Not that they could have eaten any more, but the presence of Aunt B was a protection; now they would have to face the silence of Richard and the sulkiness of Kate by themselves. They walked along the dark cold passage to the back room. They were still wearing their coats, but they shivered. The back room was lit by a gas lamp with a broken mantle that made a curious moaning noise, and there was a very small fire in the black marble fireplace, nearly out now. Richard flung himself into the only armchair and looked wearily at the three Greshams. Aunt B poked her head round the door.

'That's right, you have some nice games all together and try to get warm. Only don't you go frightening people into fits, Richie; once is enough.'

'Well,' said Richard, looking at the Greshams. 'And what sort of nice games do you propose we should play?'

There was an uncomfortable silence. Nobody could think of anything they could possibly want to do.

'Are you going to broaden our horizons?' Amy enquired. 'Because I don't want to.'

'Horizons,' said Richard broodingly, slumped in his chair. 'Well, I did my best for you Greshams, but it's been useless as far as I can see.'

'You go and broaden yours then,' said Amy aggressively.

Kate rounded on her fiercely. 'What do you mean, broaden Richard's horizons? They couldn't possibly be any wider. He knows about millions of things that you've never heard of. Don't you?' she said to Richard heatedly.

'I daresay, but that wouldn't be difficult,' said Richard with indifference.

'So you put that in your pipe and smoke it, you fat-headed little donkey.' Kate seemed really angry now.

Amy was getting roused in her turn. 'I don't know why you talk like that about us. We're just as good as you, and I bet there are all sorts of things that we can do and you can't.'

Kate was scornful. 'Such as what?'

Amy cast round wildly in her mind. 'He can't climb the tree,' she shouted. 'Nor can you. I can.'

'So could we if we wanted to. We don't want to, we think it's silly.'

'Then why did you tell Henry to before he could join your society? You don't because you're frightened. Go on, I dare you to.'

The Greshams stared apprehensively at the Holts. Amy had done it now. Everybody knew that if you were dared something, you had to do it, otherwise you were branded for ever as the lowest sort of coward. At least, that was what applied to the sort of world that the Greshams lived in. Even Amy seemed rather sobered by what she had said, and her anger subsided.

'You'll have to do it now,' she said in a detached way. 'Otherwise everyone will think you're a coward.'

Richard heaved himself out of his chair and they watched with fascinated alarm. Was he going to climb the tree now, in the dark?

'Very well, I will broaden your horizons. You Greshams think all the time about what other people think. Let me see, have you got a dressing-up box?'

CHAPTER 10

Julia and the Milkman

It was curious what power Richard had over them. Nobody thought of objecting or questioning him. They just followed him out of the room, out of the house, into the fog. Julia was frightened. She realized that Richard, for all his calmness, was really angry, and if he was going to take his revenge it would be no ordinary revenge, you could be sure of that.

Richard led the way up the tradesmen's path of number 22 to the back door, and they followed in a long line. He pushed against the back door without knocking, without referring to any of the Greshams. It was swollen with the winter damp and stuck at first, and he lurched against it impatiently with his full weight. It burst open with a rattle of the knocker and he strode into the scullery. It was quite dark here; only a line of light showed under the door of the kitchen. Richard threw open this door too. Julia, behind him, caught a glimpse of the scandalized faces of the two maids, who were sitting at the table having their tea. But Richard took no notice of them. He marched across the room to the door into the hall, and disappeared. Kate ran after him. Ellen recovered her wits.

'Well, I never saw the like for impudence,' she said. 'Coming into our kitchen as bold as brass without so much as by your leave. Who does he think he is, anyway? I tell you, Miss Julia, I'm not having it, I'll tell your ma. You know she won't have you using the back door anyway, and as for bringing your friends through!' She paused for breath.

'The bold-faced impudence!' said Mabel. 'And doesn't't

even say he's sorry either. Just look at all those foot-marks on my nice polish!'

'We're very sorry,' said Julia breathlessly. 'But we'll have to go with him.' She was panting with agitation.

'You certainly better'd go and fetch him down,' said Ellen grimly. 'He'll be in your pa's dressing-room next and then the fur will fly.'

They ran into the hall. There was a sound above of feet ascending the little flight of stairs on the landing, then these stopped.

'When you have stopped gossiping in the kitchen,' said Richard's voice coldly from the dark landing, 'per-haps you will have the goodness to come and tell us where to go.'

Panic-stricken, Julia chased up the stairs, two at a time, partly frightened that her parents would hear Richard's voice, but mostly frightened of Richard him-self.

'The dressing-up box is in the boxroom,' she said breathlessly. 'But it'll be terribly cold up there and there isn't any light.'

'Then you will have to provide some, won't you,' said Richard coolly, and marched up the attic stairs. They were covered with oilcloth and his boots made a clatter-ing noise which he did not attempt to soften. The noise rang through the house, and Julia felt certain that any moment Captain Gresham would open the drawing-room door and roar at them. Richard waited at the top of the stairs, under the skylight, which showed a pale blue square in the blackness.

'Well, where is the light?' he enquired.

The Greshams stood still on the dark steps below him. There were no gas lights up here, and even if there had been they were not allowed to light them themselves. Henry had an inspiration.

'Perhaps there's a candle in the maids' room.' He

climbed up the rest of the stairs and pushed open the door at one side of the landing. It was forbidden territory, but Henry was only thinking now of how to please Richard. He knew where the candle ought to be, he had seen it on occasions when the door had been left open. He fumbled for it on the washstand; it was there, and a box of matches beside it. He lit the candle. The flame flickered and grew longer, and showed up the two black iron bedsteads with Mabel and Ellen's morning print dresses thrown untidily down.

'How much longer have we got to wait in this fearful cold?' said Richard impatiently from the landing.

'I'm coming now.' Henry hurried out and opened the door of the boxroom on the other side of the landing. It was shrouded in dustsheets and the candlelight threw long sinister shadows on them. Julia started dragging off the covers and searching for the dressing-up box. Henry put down the candle and helped.

'You are making a mess,' remarked Amy. Nobody took any notice of her, but the mess certainly was considerable. In their frantic haste Henry and Julia were tumbling everything that was not the dressing-up box on to the floor—gladstone bags, dressing cases, a camp bed, army boots of Captain Gresham's, and a box of Christmas decorations whose lid fell off and tumbled tinsel and paper chains and little silvery balls everywhere; one crunched under Henry's foot.

'Here it is,' he said breathlessly, and pulled out a large cabin trunk from the bottom of everything else. There seemed to be some pictures piled on top, and they fell to the ground with a horrible crash of breaking glass. But Henry took no notice, he flung open the lid of the trunk and looked at Richard triumphantly. Richard picked up the candle and stalked over. He began pulling garments out of the trunk. He tossed them on the floor, a jumble of clothes, very crushed and smelling damp and disused. There were ancient ball dresses of their mother's, Great-Uncle Marshall's Inverness cape, a dress that Amy had worn when she had been a bridesmaid, a shepherdess's dress that Julia had worn at a children's fancy dress ball, shawls and necklaces that Captain Gresham had brought back from India, and right at the bottom, a pair of hunting top boots, battered and cracked. Kate pounced on these and dragged them out. The others took no notice, they were all intently watching Richard. He contemplated the clutter of clothes, turning them over with a contemptuous foot. Finally he pounced on a white bundle and shook it out. It was a white tarlatan dress in a very out of date style. Julia had once put it on when she wanted to play the part of a bride in some charades, but had taken it off because she thought it looked too ridiculous.

'Here, you Greshams who worry so much about what people think,' said Richard, 'let's see if you can broaden your horizons just a little. I dare you to put this on to-morrow morning and ride for an hour on the milkman's cart. The milkman comes at half-past nine, if you want to know. I *dare* you, mind.' He flung the dress at Julia and marched out of the room. They listened to his feet clattering down the attic stairs and then growing softer on the carpet of the landing. Finally the front door banged far below.

'There was a sort of a thing that looked like a saddle,' Kate said eagerly, rummaging in the debris on the floor.

'It was Papa's,' said Amy. 'When he had a horse.' She started turning over the piles in search of it. 'Here it is.'

'A real saddle!' Kate squatted down on the floor, awe-stricken. 'And here are the stirrups done up in this newspaper. Do you think I could borrow it, just for a little bit? There's something I want to try to do, a sort of game,' she said hesitatingly.

Nobody answered, the Greshams were all peering

through the candlelight at the crumpled white dress which Julia was holding up. Kate picked up the saddle, staggering a little under the weight. 'And perhaps I might as well take the boots as well,' she said in a casual voice. She scooped the hunting boots out of the bottom of the dressing-up box, piled them with some difficulty on top of the saddle and pushed her way out. They heard her going down the attic stairs. At the top of the stairs to the hall she seemed to drop the boots, for something thundered down in a series of appalling crashes. As the front door slammed the drawing-room door opened, and Captain Gresham's voice was heard.

'Henry, Julia. Come here at once.'

'We'll have to go,' said Henry in a panic.

'But look at all the mess,' objected Amy.

'Quick, throw it back against the wall and put the dust-sheet over it.' Henry picked up objects indiscriminately and hurled them into the shadowy corners of the room. Several Christmas decorations scrunched under his feet.

'Henry, Julia. Will you do as you are told at once, or do I have to come up to fetch you down?' Even at this distance their father's voice sounded very angry indeed.

'You go down, Henry,' Julia told him. 'I'll put the dust-sheets over.'

While Henry ran downstairs, Amy after him, she hastily spread a covering of dust-sheets over the piles. Then, with the white dress under her arm, she followed, just stopping at her bedroom door to fling the dress under her bed.

Captain Gresham was very irritable. He could not think what all the noise was about. He had thought they were supposed to be out to tea, and here they were careering up and down the stairs, hurling things about, opening the front door and slamming it. Anyone would think they were a tribe of Hottentots instead of decent civilized children. They had better bring books and sit quietly in the drawing-room until bedtime.

'You came back very early,' said their mother. 'You could have waited till Ellen came to fetch you. I hope you behaved yourself and remembered to thank Miss Holt.'

'Oh no, we never did,' said Amy, conscience-stricken.

'It's too late now,' said their father. 'I'm not going to have any more crashing on that front door tonight. Now hurry and fetch your books and close the door quietly after you.'

It was not often that they were encouraged to read, but Julia, as she sat with *The Children of the New Forest* on her knees, could not read a sentence for thinking of what she had to do tomorrow. Here was her chance to show the stuff she was made of, the greatness in her. This would prove to everybody that she was above minding what people thought of her. It would be something to be remembered when they came to write her life, and hundreds of years on, it might even be the sort of anecdote that everybody would know about her, like the story of the little Handel diligently copying out music in the secrecy of his bedroom against the wishes of his father. She was excited but appalled by what lay ahead of her. Henry was only appalled, and kept eyeing her surreptitiously under his eyelashes.

'Ju,' he said as they went upstairs to bed, 'you aren't really going to do it, are you? I'm sure Richard couldn't have meant to dare *you*. It was Amy he was so cross with, not you.'

'He meant *me*,' Julia said calmly. Richard had flung the dress at her, it was she that he had picked out for greatness, and this was his way of testing her.

Then a fearful thought came to Henry. 'But to-morrow's Sunday!'

'I will have to do it just the same,' said Julia airily.

'Sunday!' Henry repeated, shuddering. Then a ray of hope presented itself. 'Perhaps it will still be foggy. Nobody could see you if it's like today.'

But Sunday was not foggy. The heavy white swathes of mist disappeared overnight and the morning was cold and clear. As soon as she had finished breakfast Julia hurried upstairs, put on the white dress and stole furtively into her parents' bedroom to examine herself in the long glass there, hoping against hope that this time the dress would not look so ludicrous as it had the time before. But of course it did, and with its low-cut neck it looked doubly foolish on top of her Sunday green merino dress. What was more, the white of it was going to be horribly conspicuous in broad daylight. She rushed along the landing and into the spare bedroom. It overlooked the road and she could wait for the milkman there. Nobody would go into it in the normal course of events, but to guard against being seen she did what they were strictly forbidden to do in any room, she locked the door.

Everything was swathed in brown holland covers, and it was exceedingly cold. There was no sign of the milkman and she began to hope that he would not come, because if he did not, she could not possibly be blamed for not carrying out her task. But come he did; she heard the clip-clopping of his horse at the top of the road, and then it was only a question of a few minutes before he worked his way down to number 22. The cart advanced in jerks of a few yards at a time, with stops to allow the milkman to run up to the back doors of houses further up the road. He kept up a tuneless whistling all the time, hardly drawing breath except to say 'gee-up' to his horse after each stop. He came to number 22. Julia heard the slam of the gate and his feet tramping up the passage. There was a knocking in the distance, the faint sound of voices,

then he tramped back again, and the cart moved off
to number 24. It could be no longer put off now. Julia
hovered nervously on the landing; there was nobody
about. Then, holding the tarlatan high above her knees,
she plunged down the stairs, through the front door
which she closed as gently as she could, and out.

Outside the Holts' house the milkman with the dipper
in his hand was just stepping into his cart. Self-con-
sciously she walked up behind him. 'Could I come on
the cart with you?'

He turned round and stared. 'Well, I'm blessed and
whoever do you think you are? It's usually the boys as
wants to ride. And not the young gentlemen from
houses like this, neither. It's not the thing for a young
lady to be doing. Is that your ma's dress you've got
on? You'd better go and take it off, hadn't you?'

'It isn't hers, it's from the dressing-up box,' she said
desperately. 'It's a sort of dare that I wear it.' She gave a
fearful glance over her shoulder. Somebody was bound
to look out of one of the bedroom windows unless this
man hurried.

'Silly sort of dare then. Well, you can't come with me.
Besides what your ma would say, I'd never hear the
last of it from Mr Higgins at the dairy. He's a proud
man is Mr Higgins and Higgins's milk has got a good
name.'

Tears came into Julia's eyes. She had never thought
of this difficulty, she had thought that riding on the
milk cart was only a matter of asking for it. 'But please
can't I? I just must, I sort of promised I would.'

Perhaps it was the tears that made him relent. 'If
you're going to carry on like that, I suppose you must.
But only till we reach the London road, mind. And
don't you go running away with the idea that you're
going to drive. I won't let any of the boys. The mare
knows my hand and I won't answer for the consequences

if she feels another.'

Gratefully Julia climbed up into the cart which dipped under her weight, and squeezed herself against the milk-churns, hoping by this to hide some of her dress from whoever might be about at this hour on a Sunday morning. Then she remembered that Richard was probably looking out to see how she was performing her task. She threw her head back and stood erectly, feeling for a moment like Boadicea riding into battle. The milkman noticed.

'Seem to have a fine opinion of yourself, you have. Well, all I can say is that most people'd say you looked proper freakish.' He started his whistling again, and Julia, feeling furiously angry and humiliated, cowered closer to the churns.

Not many houses took Higgins's milk at this end of Clifton road, it seemed. It was a great relief, she did not want to linger in the cart with all the neighbours eyeing her from their windows. And the London road was hardly any distance away; if the milkman made her get down there, Richard could hardly blame her for not going any further. But the milkman, who had not got anything to do now except drive, turned his attention to Julia.

'It wasn't like that in my young days I can tell you,' he remarked.

'Like what?' said Julia.

'Young ladies prancing around all got-up like heathen idols. Ladies knew their place in those days. And so did we, I can tell you. Father'd have taken the strap to any of us who didn't do what we was told in a twink, like that.' He snapped his fingers. ' "Want a taste of Thomas the Tickler?" he'd say and reach for that strap behind the door. And my word, we'd fly. But it's all different now, children go round being as cheeky as they please, saying they want this thing and they don't want that, and nobody tickles them up. My word, they'd be better

for a dose of strap.' He sucked his teeth and nodded his head grimly. 'What do you say to that?' he asked suddenly.

Julia kept a haughty silence, though she clenched her fingers angrily until the nails dugs into her palms. But martyrs did not flinch, and nor would she.

'And in my young day children were taught to answer

their elders when they were spoken to,' said the milkman pointedly.

Julia controlled herself as well as she was able. 'Shall I go to this back door for you?' she said very coldly. The cart had stopped outside a large house at the top of the next road, and she thought she might as well carry her martyrdom to its utmost limit.

'Can do, if you like,' said the milkman indifferently. 'I'm a Radical, I am, and I don't see why the gentry shouldn't work just the same as us poor folk.' He leant against the churns and started whistling.

Holding her dress high, Julia jumped off the cart and went through the tradesmen's gate. Nervously she knocked at the back door and straightened herself, trying to look as unconcerned as she could. The door was pulled open by a maid who had her head turned over her shoulder, carrying on a loud conversation with somebody behind her. When she turned to look at Julia her mouth fell open.

'My eyes, and whoever are you? (Come and look, Bessie, have you ever seen the like of this?) You'd better be off, little girl, the mistress don't hold with gipsies.'

Julia's voice trembled with rage and humiliation. 'I'm helping the milkman. How much milk do you want?'

'Do you hear that?' said the maid to the other servants who were now clustering round. 'Speaks like a young lady too. Now be off with you, do, we only deal with Higgins's Dairy.'

'I am from Higgins's Dairy,' said Julia in a choked voice. 'The cart's outside, you can come and see if you like.' She forgot all about dignity and courage, and fled. The maids came after her, and when she reached the safety of the cart she turned round and faced them, like an animal at bay. The milkman stopped whistling and stared.

'What's gone wrong with them? Seem in a bit of

a hurry for your milk this morning, don't you?' he called.

'Well I never,' said the maid who had opened the door. 'It is Higgins's Dairy and all. Who's your lady friend, Mr Mallow?'

'Young lady from Clifton road way who's taken a fancy for a ride.' The milkman lifted the top off the churn. 'Beats me why she's got herself up like that. How much milk today?'

The milk was poured into the huge white jug while the maids stared at Julia and chattered. She gazed down the road and pretended not to notice, but when the milk cart finally drove off they were still clustered on the pavement, staring.

'You'll be getting me into trouble,' observed the milkman. 'You'd better stay in this cart now. Only as far as the London road, mind!'

Julia would have liked to have announced that she would get out now, but Richard had told her to stay there for an hour, and an hour she must stay, cost what it might. Or if not an hour, then until the milkman finally told her to go. The London road was in fact not very far away, but every time the cart drew near it the milkman pulled his horse round to go back along one of the labyrinthine roads that branched off each other all round this part of Melsham. The horse meandered along with its head sunk low, only breaking into a pretence of a trot when the milkman flicked his whip near its ears. Sometimes maids came to the gates with their jugs and stared curiously at Julia. But worse than that were the people who were now strolling down the roads on their way to church. Mothers and fathers with their children walking primly beside them stared at Julia and murmured among themselves—she was aware of it even though she did not look at them. Stiff and numb with cold (she was wearing no coat or gloves), she gazed straight down the road ahead over the horse's ears, thankful that she was short-sighted and could not recognize anybody. She hated the milkman, she hated his tuneless whistling, and she hated the smell of the milkchurns, she never wanted to drink a drop of milk again as long as she lived. At last the cart was in a road (the one parallel to theirs, in fact) that led directly into the London road, and where there seemed positively no turning to take them back. The milkman drew up outside a prim yellow brick house with immaculate white steps and polished brasses.

'Last one. You can do it as you're so keen. Then you've got to get off, see. Take the dipper with a pint in it and ask if they want any more, and mind you say you're from Higgins's Dairy this time.'

This house had no separate tradesmen's gate, you had to walk past the front door on the trim gravel path to reach the back entrance. Julia with numb, frozen feet, clambered up the steps to the front garden, trod on her dress, and fell heavily and painfully on her knee. However, the milk was safe, and with tears of pain blinding her eyes she scrambled up, just as an elderly lady opened the front door. Pity was the last thing she wanted, so she scuttled past to the back regions. The elderly maid who answered the door said they only wanted the pint today, and looked curiously at Julia. But she was used to that now.

'They don't want any more. Here's the dipper. Thank you for letting me come,' she said hastily to the milkman.

'All I can say is I hope it's done you some good. And you just bear in mind what I said about Thomas the Tickler. He does the young idea more good than sweetmeats and the like. By the by, do you know the party as has just come out? No? Well, it's just as well for you that you don't, I say, she looked as though she had got it in for someone.' He flicked the whip, the horse broke into a poor sort of trot and Julia ran for dear life towards home. As she rushed round the corner of Clifton road she nearly knocked someone down. She staggered and was just going to apologize when she saw it was Richard. With his hands plunged into his coat pocket and his collar turned up he was ambling along in his usual dejected way, kicking a stone in front of him.

'What's the time?' said Julia breathlessly. 'It is after half-past ten, isn't it?'

'Oh it's you, is it,' he said with no enthusiasm. 'How should I know. You ought to, your house has about six clocks in every room. We've only got Aunt B's alarm clock, and it only goes on its side.'

'But you're supposed to be timing me,' Julia screamed at him.

'Who said I'm supposed to be timing you, pray? I am merely trying to cure you Greshams of your obsession about what people think. And to teach you in particular that you don't get off so lightly from ill-treating my sister.'

'Ill-treating your sister?' She stared at him.

'Don't pretend you don't know anything about it. It was only yesterday morning. She came in crying and when I got her to say what was wrong, she mumbled something about you not letting her go in your house. And talking about your house, you'd better hurry. There seems to be a fine old rumpus going on next door.' Wriggling his shoulders and pushing his hands further into his pockets he slouched off round the corner.

Julia stared after him for a moment, then, nearly sobbing with rage, holding the dress up as best she could with her numb hands, she ran the rest of the way home. She was so angry that she envied Amy her tantrums; it would be a pleasure to lie on the floor and scream and kick.

She was within a few yards of her house when she heard the unmistakable banging of the front door. But she just ran blindly on. As she reached the gate it was opened and her father and mother came out with Amy and Henry behind.

'There she is,' announced Amy. 'She's been broadening her horizons, like I told you.'

And from behind Julia came another voice. 'Captain Gresham, I consider it my duty to speak to you about your daughter's behaviour.'

CHAPTER II

The Storm Breaks

Julia was ordered to her bedroom. She was too winded with rage and with running to take in what was happening. She was just aware of being bundled in through the front door and hearing Amy's scandalized voice saying in the background, 'But Papa will be late for church!'

'Go to your bedroom at once,' said her father when they were in the hall. She took one scared look at him and saw that the veins on his forehead were swelling, then she ran upstairs, treading again on the unfortunate dress, and sprawling headlong on the landing. She had only once or twice seen his face like that; the last time was when Henry had scribbled on the wall as a little boy and in blind terror had denied it. As she picked herself up from the landing she saw Captain Gresham going into the dining-room, and ahead of him a lady in a brown cloak. Of course, it was the Old Dame, and it was the Old Dame's house where she had finally delivered the milk.

Ellen was in the bedroom, making the bed. 'I've got to come here,' Julia said as flippantly as she could. Ellen straightened herself and stared at Julia, her hands on her hips.

'So it's you, Miss Julia, with the whole house upside down because you couldn't be found. On a Sunday too, I don't know how you could bring yourself to be so naughty. And just look at you! Well, all I can say is I hope you were clean out of your senses when you ran off like that because if you were in your right mind there's no hope for you. All right, all right, I'm going,

I'm sure I don't want to stay in the same room as such a naughty girl as you are.'

Julia sat on her bed, which was unmade. She clutched her arms round her and shivered with cold. Then she wondered whether she was supposed to go to bed or not. She decided that she probably was, it seemed more of a punishment than just being sent to her bedroom. The problem was how many clothes to take off. If you were being punished and were perfectly well it seemed wrong and a waste of time besides, to take off all your clothes and put on a nightdress. So after a moment or two of thought, she undressed as far as her flannel petticoat and pulled the icy sheet over her. Her feet seemed not to be there at all they were so cold. She hunched them up as high as she could, holding them with her hands to try to warm them.

'At any rate,' she thought, 'nobody can give anybody a row when they're in bed.' The front door opened and shut, the house became very still, nobody came to her. 'There's nobody in to row me now, and surely they can't do it directly they come back from church, that would be blasphemous.' She was not sure what this meant, but it sounded good, and it convinced her.

In fact the row did not come with the return of the family. She heard the ring at the front door, the footsteps of the maid who answered the bell, subdued voices in the hall below. Nobody came near her bedroom, she huddled there, holding her feet and listening. She could only pick out Amy's voice, and somebody quickly hushed her. A smell of roasting meat floated through the house—the kitchen door must have been opened; the gong was banged, feet went along the hall to the dining-room. Quiet hung over the house for fifteen minutes or so. 'I should think it's a grim sort of meal, nobody saying anything,' Julia said to herself. It was comforting to try to treat the matter in a light way, but when she attempted to make herself laugh by picturing the family all sitting round the table, watching her father and not daring to talk, it was a dismal failure. She thought of the veins swelling on his forehead and shivered. The bell rang from the dining-room. This meant they were ready for their pudding—it was always jelly and stewed fruit on Sundays. Footsteps went along the hall, there was a clattering of dishes, more footsteps and then silence. Evidently nobody was going to bring her any dinner.

It was her mother who finally came for her. She looked as though she had got one of her migraine headaches; she was white-faced with heavy circles under her eyes. 'You are to come down to Papa at once,' she said.

Julia peered up over the sheets. 'But I'm not dressed.'

'Don't make such stupid excuses,' said her mother sharply. 'Get up and put your clothes on.'

Julia dragged on her dress, straightened her hair, and started down the stairs. She glanced over the banisters at the schoolroom door. It was open a tiny crack; Amy must be peeping out. 'I can see you, Amy,' she said aloud, and the door was immediately closed.

It was difficult to know how to walk into the drawing-room; whether to look her father in the face or to hang her head, or what. Unfortunately in her embarrassment and confusion she smiled. It horrified her, but she could not help it; very solemn occasions always did make her want to giggle.

'Brazen defiance,' said her father icily from the hearth-rug. 'I might have expected it.'

'I didn't mean to, Papa,' she said abjectly.

'Didn't mean to! You're not an imbecile, or at least I hope you're not. I suppose you didn't *mean* to go gallivanting about the streets this morning.' Julia said nothing, not in a million years could she ever explain to her father about this test of greatness. 'Well,' said Captain Gresham, 'answer me.'

G.G.   F

She stared hopelessly back. Captain Gresham stood in front of the fire, the veins on his forehead were still swollen, he tapped an ivory paper knife on the marble of the chimney-piece. Mrs Gresham sat in her chair, she was not looking at Julia, she was staring hopelessly into the fire. Julia suddenly felt very sorry for her mother.

'I'm very sorry,' she said abjectly.

But this only increased her father's violence. 'It's no good whatever saying you're sorry when as far as I can see you'll turn round and do some other maniac thing the minute you are left alone. Do you know what Miss Moule said? She said that she did work for the Girls' Rescue Crusade and she wanted to know whether I need their help! There, what do you think of that? You, a Gresham, being classed with those abandoned girls from the poorest and worst sort of homes!'

At this point Mrs Gresham began to cry, very quietly, pressing her handkerchief against her eyes. Julia was appalled. 'It was a game,' she said feebly. 'A sort of a game.'

'I have never heard such a futile excuse,' her father shouted. 'A game, that took you out on a Sunday morning, dressed like a pantomime, to ride on the milkman's cart and bait Miss Moule. I don't know how we are to hold up our heads after this, we may have to leave the district altogether.'

Mrs Gresham spoke in a choked way through her handkerchief. 'And to go out in my old ball-dress, too, my coming-out dress! To make a guy of *me*, Julia! How could you have done it? In a milkman's cart!' Her crying became audible now, and she blew her nose loudly.

'Mamma, I never knew,' said Julia horrified. 'It was in the dressing-up box, I never thought whose it was.'

'Never mind whose dress it was,' Captain Gresham said impatiently. 'What I'm going to say to you now,

Julia, is far more serious than any of this tomfoolery. I want to know just what was going on three months ago that Miss Moule should meet you in a railway carriage, coming back from London, in the company of some ruffianly children, and reading a book that no lady should even have heard of.'

Julia was stupefied, and could not find her wits or her voice to answer. Her first thought was the unfairness of it—why, it had been over and done with for months! When she spoke at last, her voice was shrill with indignation. 'But you knew all about it, Papa. It was that night when you looked out of the window and saw Henry climbing the apple tree.'

Captain Gresham flung down the paper knife and stamped on the hearthrug. 'Don't you dare tell me that I knew about it, Julia. Alone in a railway carriage, reading *Don Juan*! How could I have heard about it and said nothing to you! Miss Moule even said that she had heard you had been riding in a hansom cab.'

Outraged by the injustice of it all, Julia appealed to her mother. 'Mamma, you say. Miss Moule told you and you told Papa, didn't you?'

Mrs Gresham lifted a tear-stained face from her hand-kerchief. 'I started to tell you, Frank; but so many things happened that night. We were going out to the Webbs for dinner, and then Amy was lost, and as I was talking you looked out of the window and saw Henry. Perhaps you did not hear what I was saying.'

'All I heard was some story about Julia running around with some children. But as for a hansom cab and *Don Juan* . . . !' Words failed Captain Gresham, and he almost choked.

Mrs Gresham bowed her head and spoke into her handkerchief. 'I couldn't bring myself to talk about it.'

'Do you see what you have done?' Captain Gresham said icily to Julia. 'You have done things that your

mother cannot even bear to mention. You are no longer
fit to associate with your brother and sister. You had
better stay in your bedroom until further notice. I will
send a note to your school. And I don't know who those
children are that you have been consorting with, but I
forbid you ever to go with them again. You can go up
now.'

Julia went out of the room. It was unfortunate that
the door handle slipped out of her hand and the door
slammed shut. 'I'm sorry,' she called through it, but
nobody answered. The schoolroom door opened softly,
and Amy peered out. 'Was Papa very angry?' she whispered ghoulishly. 'We could hear him stamping.'

'You had better not talk to me, I'm not fit to associate
with you,' Julia said.

The drawing-room door was snatched open. 'Julia, I
will not have this insolence,' her father roared at her.
Frightened, Julia scuffled upstairs.

She was not kept in the bedroom long; after all, it was
Amy's bedroom too, and she was to be kept away
from Amy and Henry. Ellen was sent upstairs to move
her to the spare bedroom. She had clearly been told
not to talk to Julia, and anyway she was cross, Julia
knew, at having to come upstairs into the cold when
she might have been sitting by the kitchen fire and
crying over *The Wide Wide World*. With a grim face
Ellen whipped the dustsheets off the spare bed and one
of the chairs, laid and lit the fire, slammed down a tray
with a glass of milk and some bread and butter on it, and
went out, first removing the key from the door and
locking it on the outside.

Julia had been rather pleased, in spite of herself, with
the dramatic way she was being punished. To take her
away from school too! But when she heard the key
turning in the lock her spirits sank. It was so bitterly
cold, and she hated the spare room, with its gloomy

purple wallpaper patterned with blue leaves, and the maroon coloured paint. There was also the long glass in the wardrobe which you would look up at suddenly and see yourself watching yourself, or else catch sight of the reflection from the corner of your eye and fancy for a second that there was somebody else in the room. There were a few books, but nothing that anybody could conceivably want to read. There was a manual of military law, a German dictionary, a book about fencing and something called *Thoughts on the Apocalypse*. The only reason why these were in the spare room at all seemed to be that they fitted into the fretwork bookholder on the chest of drawers.

There were more voices and the front door slammed. Papa was taking Henry and Amy for the Sunday afternoon walk; she watched their backs going down the road. They were not out for long, she was still at the window when they came up the road, and ducked hastily so that they would not see her. Footsteps came up the stairs a few minutes later, hesitated, and then tiptoed down the passage that led to the spare room. There was hard breathing outside.

'Who's that?' Julia called. But nobody answered. A minute or two later there was a rustling sound on the floorboards, and a piece of paper was pushed underneath.

'Papa says we cannot talk to you or go in but he did not say we could not write. It is very horrid downstairs he is so cross. Are you all right? Your affectionate brother Henry.'

'Yes, I'm all right,' she said aloud. 'But it's cold and here's nothing to do. Nothing to read, even.'

Downstairs somebody was moving in the hall. The breathing outside the spare room door stopped, and she heard steps scuttling away. 'Little coward,' she thought contemptuously, and threw herself moodily on the bed. It began to get dark, but nobody came to light the gas or bring her any tea. She was staring from the bed at the lamp in the street which had just been lit when she heard a scratching noise at the door. Alarmed, she propped herself on her elbow and peered down. A white rectangle slowly made its way under the door. At first she was frightened and stared at the slowly moving white patch, then she jumped down and grabbed it. It was a magazine, Henry's *Boy's Own Paper*, and there was a note lying on it.

'This is all I can find that will fit under the door. You can have *Chatterbox* tomorrow when Amy finishes it. I know we are not meant to read magazines on Sunday but I can't get books through they are too big. Your affectionate bro. Henry.'

'Thank you very much,' said Julia to the empty air. She poked the fire into a little more life, and settled down to try to read by its light. However, Mabel came up soon afterwards with more bread and butter, and a bowl of prunes, and she lit the gas. Julia toasted the bread and butter at the fire (it was not really hot enough to toast it, but it gave the bread a pleasant smoky flavour), spread it with mashed prunes, and sipped her milk and read the *Boy's Own Paper*, dripping butter and prune juice on to the pages. It had never been possible to read with her meals before, and she told herself she was really very happy and comfortable.

The next day passed very slowly. Henry and Amy were, of course, away at school all day, and Julia had long ago extracted every single word there was to read in Henry's magazine. Towards the middle of the morning her mother came in with a pile of pillowcases and table napkins that she told Julia to mend. She also brou h a Bible and a Prayer Book. She put them all down on the chest of drawers and faced Julia.

'Who is responsible for the disgraceful state of the boxroom?'

'I'm afraid we did make rather a mess,' said Julia guiltily.

Her mother spoke with a trembling voice. 'Julia, how can you be so irresponsible and thoughtless? It will take a whole morning to put right again and Ellen is so busy. And I will have to be up there with her to show her where things go.'

Julia felt ashamed. 'I'm very sorry, Mamma. I'll go up and tidy it.' But her mother had gone from the room even while she was speaking.

Henry brought news of more disasters downstairs that night before he went to bed. He pushed a hastily scribbled note under the door, together with a copy of *Our Boys* which he had managed to borrow from a friend at school.

'Dear Julia. P. is very angry because of what we did to the boxroom. Amy and I did not tell him who did it but Ellen told M. about Richard and Cate coming through the kitchen yesterday so P. got very ragey and said we must never play with them. But Cate has got P's saddle what are we going to do? In haste, yours, Henry.'

Julia heard more about it that evening. Her father unlocked the door and strode in. She had enough warning to throw *Our Boys* under the bed and pick up some mending.

'Julia, I hear the children from the next door house broke into the kitchen last night. I don't know who they are or how you have come to know them, but I will not have any more of it. They must never come to this

house again, do you understand? Nor are you to go into
theirs. I suppose they must be the children that Miss
Moule saw you with. She told me they were insolent,
rude and aggressive, and they certainly seem to have
succeeded in making you the same. I cannot understand
how you ever came to know them in the first place.'

'Mamma asked them to tea.' Julia was so indignant
that she forgot all prudence. 'And you saw us playing
in their garden yourself.'

'Julia, your insolence is beyond bearing!' Her father
stormed out of the room.

This interview left Julia rather elated. Here was
persecution. She was being shut up because she had
read a book her father disapproved of, and because she
had been friendly with the Holts. She began to feel
like a mixture of the young Handel and of Juliet in the
story of *Romeo and Juliet* which she had read in *Lamb's
Tales from Shakespeare*. There is something very time-
consuming about having a grudge, and time was something that Julia just now had plenty of. She whiled
away hours while she might have been darning the linen
for her mother, brooding over her wrongs. She did
wish, though, that she knew what *Don Juan* was about.
It did seem such a waste getting into this fearful trouble
when she had not read a word of it.

By the fourth day of her imprisonment, Wednesday,
her spirits were getting rather low. It was all very well
to be a martyr, but she was not clear what she was
being martyred for, and she still had got no further in
deciding what she was going to be great *at*. There was
also at the back of her mind the recollection that her
last task as a member of the SAGBOHEICIM seemed not
to have been set so much as a task as for a punishment.
But unexpectedly, Henry restored her faith in herself.
He came in early that afternoon (Wednesday was always

a half-holiday at his school), and crept up to the spare room at once. A note came sliding under the door.

> 'Dear Julia, I have got a present. If I unlock the door will you open it. Papa did not tell you not to open it did he? Your affectionate brother, Henry. P.S. I do not know about the other book but it was all Mr Kirkshaw had in the shop for 1d.'

When the door was unlocked, Julia opened it a crack. From the other side Henry, still unseen, pushed round the door two rather battered books. Julia fell on them like a famished castaway. One was called *Wanderings in Westminster* and was full of little drawings of old buildings and arches and tombs. Its cover was hanging off and some of its pages were loose, but it looked enthralling. The other book seemed to be the one that was all Henry could buy for a penny. You could no longer read the title on the spine because it was so worn, but the title pages said *Examples for Youth, in Remarkable Instances of Early Piety*. It had an interesting picture opposite of a young man in a dressing-gown and nightcap, sitting in an armchair, dying, watched by some children, and the date was 1822.

'Henry, you are a darling,' said Julia, deeply touched. 'You really are.' All his weekend pocket money must have gone on this present, and the buying of it must have needed great courage, for Henry hated going into shops by himself, and Mr Kirkshaw in particular was a surly old man who disliked schoolboys lingering by the tables of books that he displayed just inside his door.

'I thought you might like them if you've got nothing to read,' said Henry, and then, realizing that he had talked to Julia when he had been forbidden to, he ran away.

Julia settled with the books in front of her wretched glimmer of a fire. After so long without anything, it seemed a feast, and she did not know which to start upon, but kept dipping first into one, then into another, reading snatches and looking at the pictures. *Examples for Youth* had fascinating pictures of deathbeds, and it was very interesting to see what the children had died of. Then she discovered that *Wanderings in Westminster* of course dealt with Westminster Abbey—'this hallowed fane, the temple of kings' was how the author referred to it. She gobbled it up, delighted when he described things that she remembered, though she found to her grief that there was a tremendous amount that she had missed. Towards the end of the chapter that dealt with the abbey the author quoted an epitaph:

'*What so thou hast of nature, or of Arts,*
 Youth, Beautie, Strength, or what excellent parts
 Of Mynd and Boddie, Letters, Arms and Worth,
 His Eighteene Yeares, beyond his Yeares, Brought Forth.
 Then Stand and Read Thy Self Within this Glas
 How Soone Theise Perish and Thy Self May Pas.

Man's Life is Measured by the Worke not Dayes
No Aged Sloth but Active Youth hath Prayse.'

Great tears rolled slowly down Julia's cheeks and trickled into her mouth. She was not entirely clear what this meant, except that the young man had died young, aged eighteen. This then was a way to achieve greatness, to die young, lamented by everybody. 'Being fnatch'd away fuddenly by Death', quoted the author from another inscription (where the s's were all printed like f's), 'which he had long meditated and expected with conftancy. His Heart was as truly Great and Noble as His High Defcent.' Light broke upon Julia. She might yet be buried in Westminster Abbey if she died young enough and good enough, and if she could do it by meditating on death with constancy, well, that was what she would do. She would set to at once, and she got up, fetched the Prayer Book her mother had left with her, and turned to the Burial of the Dead. Then she remembered Henry's penny book, *Remarkable Instances of Early Piety*. Of course this was the guidebook for her.

She began with the children of eight and nine years old. She was ashamed to see how pious they were and what an enormous way she had to go. 'If I should live till I am older,' said Mary Post aged eight, 'the devil may tempt me to be naughty, and I might offend the Lord.' Julia read right through the book until it dealt with people of nineteen and twenty, an age she reckoned to be young no longer, it was easy enough to be good and pious when you were grownup. All the children were obedient and sweet-natured and resigned to their fates, and she realized she must no longer be rebellious towards her father. Well, it would be a great sacrifice, especially when he could be unfair and make wrongful accusations, but if she was going to be buried in Westminster Abbey because of her godliness, she would have to start at once. She started to study the service for the Burial of the Dead again, and was weeping over it, imagining herself in the coffin, when her mother brought up her tea.

CHAPTER 12

The Libation

It was the tears that she shed over the Burial service that restored Julia to her family. Her mother came in unexpectedly, and Julia raised a tear-stained face and blinked at her through watery eyes. She had not done it on purpose, but it could not have been a better moment. Her mother gave one glance at the Prayer Book that Julia was holding, and hurried out of the room. A few minutes later her father, who had just come in from the City, came up to her.

'I am very glad to hear that you have come to your right mind at last. Now, will you promise me on your word of honour as a Gresham that this sort of thing will never, never happen again?'

Julia, with all the examples of early piety in her mind, bowed her head and said 'Yes, Papa', with the greatest possible meekness. Then, feeling that perhaps she ought to go a little further, and remembering some of the old-fashioned children's books she had read, she fell on her knees and said 'Forgive me, Papa.' (She rather thought that Lucy and Henry Fairchild had once done this.)

Her father seemed a little embarrassed. He came over to her. 'Come, come, Julia, you can get up. Well, we'll say no more about it now and you may come down-stairs again.' He scraped his whiskers over her forehead, which was his way of kissing, and Julia went out of the door into freedom.

It was odd seeing the house again and noticing the small changes that had been made during her captivity. The position of ornaments in the drawing-room had been altered, there was a new plant there, a different

sort of biscuit in the biscuit barrel in the dining-room,
and Ellen had hung up a calendar in the kitchen. Henry
seemed pleased to see her, but Amy said she had liked
having the bedroom to herself and wished she could
always. Julia was going to say something sharp. Then
she remembered her new ambition and said, 'It will
be yours for ever when I am dead.'

'But that won't be for a long time,' said Amy disconsolately.

'It may be sooner than you think,' Julia said in a melancholy voice.

It was disappointing at school. Nobody seemed to have noticed that she had been away, and none of the girls questioned her. The mistresses might have been told of her captivity, but they did not mention it, and she merely found that everybody had been taught about the use of the subjunctive in French and were busy translating sentences with subjunctives in them which she could not tackle. So she sat and dreamed about her funeral service in Westminster Abbey, and the yards and yards of black crape that everybody would wear, and the guard of honour that the girls of Holly Bank would form, all in the deepest black with enormous black handkerchiefs. Of course she got into trouble for dreaming, and realized with a jerk that she had already been led astray from her determination to be pious and dutiful. So she sat with her eyes anxiously glued on the French mistress, her hands folded demurely in her lap, and did not learn much more about the subjunctive that way, either.

As the weeks went by she found the piety harder and harder to keep up. She did not see how anybody could be sweet and long-suffering where Amy was concerned (besides it would be very bad for Amy's character). And though she pored over *Remarkable Instances*, it did not give her very much help about what she should do now. It dealt almost entirely with the last days of children, so that she was very well acquainted with what she should say when she was dying, but not at all clear how she should be behaving now. She did, however, put on an air of great meekness when her father was about. This was easier to keep up, because she did not see him so very often, and also because she enjoyed his rather embarrassed look when she said things like 'Yes, indeed, dear Papa, let it be as you will.' Amy once or twice opened her eyes wide and said wasn't Julia funny, but her father told her quite sharply not to interfere. This was an event, for Amy the favourite to be out of favour. However, Julia thought that she was slipping away from her high ideals, and to try to bring herself back she wrote in capital letters at the top of each day's entry in her diary: 'N.B. I WILL BE GREAT. I WILL MEDITATE ON DEATH WITH CONFTANCY.'

(Of course, she knew it should really be an 's', but the old-fashioned 'f' shaped 's' made it sound splendidly impressive in a muffled sort of way.)

The icy cold January was succeeded by an even colder February. The snow that fell at the beginning of the month froze and lay on the ground for weeks on end. Then March came and brought with it torrential rain. They never saw the Holts now, they had forgotten even to think about them, and indeed when you hurried through this sort of weather on your way to and from school it was difficult to think about anything except how cold or how wet it was. But at last towards the end of March it became possible to realize that perhaps the spring might come. The buds on the pear tree at the corner of Clifton road seemed to be larger, there was a bird singing, and the ancient hawthorn tree in the next road showed tiny points of green.

Best of all, the Easter holidays were approaching. Easter was late that year, not till the middle of April, and the term was dragging wearily. There had been an epidemic of measles. The Greshams had not caught it, but most of their friends had, the classes had been very low in numbers, the people who taught them seemed particularly irritable, and because of the weather they had been kept in their classrooms all day. But the beginning of April brought better weather, and the Greshams looked forward to the holidays almost with frenzy. Henry even counted the hours on a big chart that he had made. April also brought spring-cleaning. Not that they saw much of it for it was done a room at a time while they were at school, and they would come back to a scrubbed smell, a damp feeling in the air, the windows flung open, and a chill wind blowing the newly hung curtains.

On the day the holidays started they all came back from school soon after dinner. Amy and Julia rushed joyfully into the schoolroom, flinging down shoebags and satchels and outdoor clothes. Ellen, who was standing on top of the step-ladder, struggling to hang up a curtain, looked down disapprovingly.

'Now pick up that shoebag, Miss Julia, the floor's no place for it. Why we bother with spring-cleaning this schoolroom I can't think, the mess you have it in the minute the holidays start.'

'Is all the spring-cleaning done now?' said Henry listlessly from the chair he had thrown himself into. He disliked it, it meant that the maids were short-tempered, that the children were in the way wherever they went, and that Mabel did not have time to cook proper meals— you had to eat cold meat until the joint was finished up instead of having shepherd's pie on the third day.

'All done bar the boxroom,' said Ellen with satisfaction. 'And that will have to wait until the holidays are over. There's no time for anything with all you children all over the place. Well, Master Henry, aren't you going to put the last red ticks in that chart of yours? The holidays are with us now.' The curtains were hung at last, she was folding up the ladders and was in a kindlier mood.

Henry looked languidly at the enormous piece of paper splattered with red ticks which was pinned on the wall beside the fireplace. 'Oh I don't know, there isn't much point now.'

'Goodness me, you aren't very lively today, are you.

Well, you'd best be stirring yourself, and don't you go taking off your coat, Miss Julia, and running away to read. Your ma'll be ready for you any minute now to go down to Charlwood's and choose your cakes for tea.'

It was a Gresham tradition that on the first afternoon of the holidays their mother should take them to Charlwood's the confectioner's and they could each choose something for tea. (It was, of course, accepted that they should choose from the buns and plainer cakes, and even Amy would not have dreamt of picking from one of the trays of eclairs, meringues, and cream-filled cakes.

'I wish we hadn't got to go,' Henry said wearily. 'The wind's so cold, it blows right through to my skin.'

Ellen was brisk. 'Get along with you. You'll feel all right when you get to Charlwood's. What's it going to be this time, Master Henry? One of those nice Chelsea buns?'

But Henry was silent. He could not believe that he had ever really enjoyed this expedition to Charlwood's. Amy and Julia, however, were in high spirits as they went down Station road with their mother. It was not so much the cake they were going to choose as the holidays beginning, whole oceans of time stretching ahead of them. They chattered animatedly and felt at peace with all the world, even with Henry, who was dragging behind and looking rather morose.

It was always fun going into Charlwood's. It was the best pastry cook's in Melsham and even to go into it gave you the feeling of being among the best people. Beyond the shop, through an arch, richly dressed ladies could be seen delicately eating pastries with forks and sipping sherry. Their furs and parcels lay on little gold-painted chairs beside them, and there was a hum of voices and a tinkling of china and much bustling of waitresses. You could not stand and stare through the arch, but what was just as good, you could stare into the enormous mirrors that lined the walls and see everything that went on there behind you. The shop was full and Julia was staring into the mirror as usual when she saw Henry, beside her, stiffen. He tugged at her elbow.

'It's Kate. She's just come into the shop. What are we going to do?'

'Talk to her, I suppose. Papa didn't say we couldn't.'

'But what about Mamma? And Ju, I've just thought. She's still got his saddle. We must get it back before Mabel spring cleans the boxroom, she always polishes the saddle then and shows it to Papa. *You* ask her.'

But Kate had seen them and came over. 'Hullo,' she said in her short, awkward way. Henry looked uneasily at his mother, but she had just found an acquaintance and was talking hard about the quality of the bombazine at Jones's the drapers.

Embarrassment made Henry chatter. 'Are you buying cakes too? We always come here the day school ends to choose a cake for tea. I don't know what I'm going to have but Julia usually has a Belgian bun and Amy usually has sponge fingers because you get a lot of those for your money, and she likes being able to eat her cake while everybody else has finished theirs.' He had said all this at top speed and now stopped, panting.

Kate pulled a half-crown out of her pocket and looked at it. 'Aunt B gave me this and told me to buy what I liked with it, something to cheer Richard up. Only it won't of course. Aunt B thinks that you can cheer anybody up with cakes. She just doesn't understand Richard.'

'Is it that he's working so hard?' Henry ventured.

'He's nearly off his head,' Kate said darkly. 'The exam's at the beginning of May.'

'I do hope he gets his scholarship,' said Julia rather weakly. She felt she ought to say something, but she was finding it difficult to look Kate in the face, remembering Richard's accusations about treating Kate badly.

'Hope!' Kate sounded savage. 'I don't know what's going to happen if he doesn't, I'm sure. I should think he'll probably kill himself. And I've taken a vow. If he does get it I'm going to give forty candles to the church. And if he doesn't I'm going to pull out all my teeth.'

'Forty candles to the church?' Henry was puzzled. 'What for?'

'That's what people do in books about olden times.'

'Will you pull out all your teeth yourself?' enquired Amy, with deep interest. 'Or will you ask a dentist to do it? I wonder how much it will cost. Perhaps you could sell the teeth.'

Kate ignored her. 'I tell you what we could do. We could have a meeting, a party of the SAGBOHEICIM, specially for him before he goes down to Christ's for the scholarship. I mean, he's the one that's going to be great and we're his society so we ought to do something about it.'

Henry looked uneasily at Julia. Surely she would explain that it was impossible. But Julia seemed to be looking over her shoulder towards her mother. 'I don't think . . .' he began. Then Julia interrupted.

'When is Richard's scholarship?'

'May 10. We could have the party the day before,' said Kate eagerly. 'And do something really special. Not just cakes like Aunt B.' She was interrupted here by a shop assistant who wanted to know if she was by herself or with the other little ladies and gentleman. With a lordly air Kate stepped forward and began pointing out the cakes and tarts that she wanted. At the same moment Mrs Gresham finished her talk with Mrs

Norman-Walker, both deciding that nothing could beat Jones's bombazine, certainly none of the big London shops supplied a better quality. She looked round to gather up the children and to settle the question of what they wanted for their tea. Then her eye fell on Kate.

'Is that the little girl from next door?' she asked in an undertone.

'She's buying cakes for her brother who's going to Christ's,' Amy informed her.

All Mrs Gresham said was, 'Now hurry up and choose your cakes, and Amy, I do hope you aren't going to dawdle like you usually do.' But Julia thought that her eye rested on Kate with a new interest.

'Are you going to go to Kate's party?' Amy demanded as soon as they got home.

'I don't know,' Julia said loftily. She realized that she should have told Kate at once that they could not. But as she had not she was forced to pretend to Amy that she was considering the question.

Henry was looking at her with horror and dismay. 'You *can't*, not after all Papa said. You should have said. And you never asked about the saddle. What are we going to do?'

'Henry's crying.' Amy peered at him with great interest. 'Whatever for?'

With both Julia and Amy staring at him, Henry could keep back the tears no longer. He put his head down on the arm of the chair and sobbed. It was Amy who sensed that something really was wrong, and she went to the schoolroom door and shouted for somebody to come, Henry was feeling ill.

Henry was put to bed with what they called at the time 'a feverish cold', but three or four days later it became quite clear that it was measles. He had it badly, he was very feverish, his eyes hurt him and he coughed all the time. Julia and Amy, who had not had measles before, were kept from him and from meeting any other children, and with the prospect of all the holidays ahead of them and no company but each other were decidedly cross. Julia would not have minded if she had been left alone to read, but Amy kept interrupting and wanting her to do things. And above all she asked with fiendish persistence, was Julia really going to go to Kate's party. Julia always answered that she had not made up her mind yet, and raged inwardly. If only Amy would forget about it. A lot of things would probably happen before May 10, which was weeks away, and anyway, Kate herself might never think any more about it.

One of the things that did in fact happen towards the middle of the holidays was that Amy got chicken pox. Nobody knew where she got it from and for the first few days, of course, they thought she was sickening for measles. Amy did not have it badly at all, though she complained loudly about how much her spots tickled her and kept on getting out of bed to examine them in the glass. During the few days that she stayed in bed Julia was left in peace to read as much as she liked. But it was not long before Amy, still very spotty and pock-marked, was allowed downstairs (Julia and Henry had had chicken-pox together years before) and sat in the schoolroom in a bored and troublesome mood. She stared at Julia and asked her every hour whether she thought she was getting measles until Julia wanted to hit her. The holidays were by now nearly over. The weather was mild and warm, there was a smell of spring in the air, and the days were passing entirely wasted. Julia felt almost smothered by the sickroom atmosphere, and the house and the small garden seemed like a prison. She would only come out of the measles quarantine a few days before the beginning of term, but for once in her life she was aching to get back to school and to throw off her imprisonment.

When Henry was no longer infectious, he left his bedroom and sat in a chair by the schoolroom fire. But he was not much company, he was in low spirits and said very little, just lying back listlessly in his chair with a magazine on his lap which he could not even be bothered to read.

They were all three of them in the schoolroom, cross, dispirited and bored, one mild May evening when their father came in to say goodbye. Every year in early summer he went up to Scotland to spend two weeks with Great-Uncle Edward who lived near Inverness. Nobody ever went with him, not even Mrs Gresham, because Uncle Edward was very old and disliked children, and being a bachelor he did not know how to entertain ladies. Captain Gresham always seemed to enjoy these visits very much, though he said they were dull, and he used to come back in high spirits with presents for them all : tartan shawls and scarves, cairngorm brooches, and sometimes, Edinburgh rock.

He scraped his whiskers over Julia and Amy and patted Henry on the shoulder. 'Now be good children and don't plague Mamma. And don't go catching any more spots while I'm away. Well, Henry, I'll expect to see you in better form when I come back. Eat a bit more and try and work up an appetite—your mother says you're hardly swallowing enough to keep a mouse alive. Oh Julia, this seems to be for you. Found it in the letterbox when I came in. What does SAGBOHEICIM mean?' But he did not wait for an answer. Ellen came to tell him that the fly was waiting to take him to the station, and with a hasty goodbye he went off, on his way to King's Cross to catch the night train to Inverness. Julia, with a very red face, was left staring at the rather dirty and crumpled envelope which said 'Miss Julia

Louise Gresham' on it, and at the bottom, SAGBOHEICIM.

Amy rushed over and stared at the writing. 'It must be from Kate. About that party. Go on, aren't you going to open it.'

Julia tore it open. Inside was a scrap of lined paper that had been torn from an exercise book.

'A meeting of the SAGBOHEICIM will be held tomorrow at half-past six at 24 Clifton road. Yours faithfully, Catherine Mary Jocelyn Holt. P.S. There will be sacrifices and you *all* must come, even Amy.' Amy read this out and then looked at Julia with round eyes. 'But Papa said we weren't to play with them.'

'You can't anyway,' Julia told her crushingly. 'You've still got chicken-pox and half-past six is your bedtime.'

'Are you going to then?'

Julia was in a dilemma. Her pride did not want her to admit to Kate that they had been forbidden, besides, here was Amy almost driving her into it by her questions. 'I don't know,' she said finally. 'I'll have to see.'

'Is it going to be a party like Kate said? Are you going to wear your best muslin and the pink sash? Will you get Mabel to call for you?'

'It's not that sort of party,' Julia said angrily. She felt it was very hard that Amy was forcing her, in spite of herself, out of the role of the dutiful, pious daughter into the role of the rebel again. The next day came, and still she had not decided what she was going to say to Kate. She was reading *The Lances of Lynwood*, and she kept putting off the writing of a note to Kate, and picking up the book instead, and then finding it was time for the next meal.

'Haven't you replied *yet*?' said Amy after tea. 'Mamma says you have to answer invitations the minute they come.'

'Oh it isn't that sort of invitation,' said Julia irritably, and reached out her hand for *The Lances of Lynwood* again. This time she was jolted out of it, not by Ellen calling her to a meal, but by the sound of Kate's voice from behind the hedge, droning 'Julia, Henry, can you come now?'

Henry was sitting up in his chair, stiff with alarm. 'Quick, go and stop her. Someone will hear her.'

'I'm going to see from the bedroom window,' said Amy darting off.

Julia went to the furthest corner of the garden and squeezed herself into the gap between the wall and the hedge. 'Hullo,' she said softly through the fence.

Kate sounded aggrieved. 'It's our party for Richard. Didn't you get my letter?'

'Yes, but it isn't half-past six yet, is it?' said Julia guiltily.

'No, I know, but we've got to get things ready. Richard's going to offer a sacrifice to the gods, or something, and we've got to collect the stuff for it. You are all going to come, aren't you? It's very important that all the Society should be there.'

Julia swallowed. 'Amy can't, she's still got her chicken-pox spots. Anyway, it's her bedtime.'

'I suppose we can do without Amy. She's a nuisance anyway.'

'What about us? Mightn't we give you chicken-pox? We've been with Amy all the time.' As she said this Julia felt a terrible cheat. Henry and she had had chicken-pox, and nobody thought that they could give it to other children, otherwise, why was she being allowed to go back to school?

There was a long pause on the other side of the fence. 'It doesn't matter about me. But do you mean you could give it to Richard? If he missed the scholarship because of chicken-pox I'd pull out all your teeth as well as mine.'

In her heart Julia knew perfectly well that it was

impossible for Richard to miss the scholarship through chicken-pox caught off either her or Henry, but she tried to persuade herself that it was a risk. 'Perhaps it would be safest for us not to come. I mean, it would be awful if anything happened to Richard.'

It might have been that Kate detected the relief in Julia's voice at having found an easy way out of her difficulty. Anyway, she became suddenly angry. 'You Greshams are hopeless, always ill or having fits or something.'

Julia defended herself. 'I can't help it about the chicken-pox. Henry's had measles, too.'

There was a noise of the Holts' garden door opening. You could not mistake it, the knocker always rattled. 'Richard,' Kate shouted. 'None of those awful Greshams can come, they've all got chicken-pox or something.'

'Plague-ridden, are they?' said Richard. He sounded in surprisingly good spirits. 'I tell you what, that hedge must be a pretty good plague-barrier. You stay on your side of it and put cloths steeped in vinegar round your mouths and I'll make a sacrifice to the gods on the other side.'

'Cloths steeped in vinegar?' Julia was out of her depth.

'A plague precaution.'

'It's something out of a book,' Kate said loftily. 'Old St. Paul's it's called. All about the plague and red crosses on the door and people shouting "Bring out your dead." We used to play it when we were children.'

'Don't alarm the poor little Greshams unduly. Now listen, you Greshams, I shall light the fire in five minutes. I shall expect ingredients for the sacrifice to be passed through the plague-barrier.'

'What sort of ingredients?' Julia asked nervously.

'Well, I don't mean a kid or a cockerel or a fatted calf. Anything you can wheedle out of your devoted retainers—flour, sugar, and so on. We'll pour out a libation to the gods.'

'Richard's just like he used to be,' Julia announced to Henry, when she had explained how easily they had solved the difficulty about attending the sacrifice. 'And we won't be disobeying Papa. We'll still be in our own garden and they'll be in theirs. You are going to come, aren't you?'

'Papa said we weren't to play with them,' said Henry tonelessly. 'Anyway, I've got a headache.'

He looked indeed as though he had one of his bad headaches. His face was white and there were dark circles under his eyes. But Julia worked herself up into a state of anger with him, partly because she was feeling guilty about having cheated over the chicken-pox danger. 'It won't be playing with them. They'll be in their garden and we'll be in ours, you've only got to come to the fence. Henry, you just must, Kate says the sacrifice won't work unless we're all there, and Amy's out of it already.'

'No,' said Henry flatly.

'You're just like Kate said,' Julia flashed in anger. 'Always ill or having fits or crying or something. You're a rotten little coward, you just have headaches when you don't want to do something. You're afraid because you remember what an idiot you were last time there was a sacrifice.'

She flounced out of the room and banged the door behind her. It was no good going to Mabel for materials for the sacrifice, but by this time she was feeling thoroughly reckless. She stole two biscuits from the biscuit barrel on the dining-room sideboard, took a cracked cup from the pantry and poured into it Worcester sauce, some oil and some vinegar. Then she crept upstairs to the medicine chest in her mother's room and tipped into the cup a drop or so from the little

bottle of brandy kept there for the direst emergencies.
(Henry sometimes had a teaspoonful if he had a very
bad bilious headache.) Finally, she wandered out into
the garden, trying to look as though she was doing
nothing in particular, and sheltering the cup with a
handkerchief.

She could hear people moving about the next garden,
the crackling of twigs and the rustling of newspapers.

'Henry can't come, he's got a headache or something,'
Julia called in a low voice. Then she added hastily to take
the edge off Kate's wrath. 'But I've got some brandy
for the sacrifice.'

She was flattered at the effect this had. Kate gave a
joyful shriek. 'Richard, some brandy! That'll make the
sacrifice work, won't it, even though the Greshams
won't come? Here, hand it over, let me see.'

Gingerly, Julia lifted the cup over the hedge. A grimy
hand stretched up and snatched it from her. Then Julia
managed to find a hole in the thick hedge so that she
could see what was going on. Kate, with great reverence,
was handing the cup to Richard, who stood by a
mountain of crumpled newspaper. He sniffed.

'It's a smelly sort of brandy. Take it away, it makes
me swoon.'

'I put some Worcester sauce in it,' Julia admitted.

'So that's what it is. Let's hope the gods can't taste or
smell. Still, perhaps they'll appreciate Gresham good
intentions. Woggle, some more newspapers from the
shed.'

Kate turned and ran. Richard busied himself with
crumpling up papers from the bundle that lay beside
him. 'This is going to be a quick fire and a good fire,' he
remarked. 'A funeral pyre of Father's hoarding over the
years. That's enough now, Woggle,' he called to Kate
who was staggering out with a slab of yellowing newspapers tied up with string. 'Stand back while I set fire.

Father always said these papers would be useful one day. They're more useful than he ever could have guessed.'

He struck a match and put it against the newspaper. The paper curled and the flame ran up it with a small thread of blue smoke. Then flames sprang up from all over the pile. Kate gave a wild whoop and flung on the slab of papers without bothering to crumple them, but after a minute the flames began to devour this too. She shrieked with delight and began dancing round the fire.

'Dear little Woggle,' said Richard. 'So impulsive.' He seemed back in the benevolent elder brother mood of the old days when he had not been made miserable by the scholarship and too much work. Julia felt very nostalgic, and longed to be dancing round the fire too. Richard was mixing things in a black urn-shaped pot that Julia, though she could not see it very clearly, thought she recognized as an ornament off the back room mantelpiece. He poured in Julia's contributions, stirring vigorously with a pencil, added things from his pockets and from a saucer on the ground. Then he held it out over the flames.

'A sacrifice,' he shouted. 'Let us appease the gods with a libation. Gather round and drink, all ye faithful, drink deep of the draught. Summon the Greshams to the plague-barrier.'

He handed the black urn to Kate, who lifted it to her lips and took a mouthful. She made a terrible face and opened her mouth wide as though it burned.

'Fortitude, my Woggle,' called Richard. 'This is a drink of the gods. Bear it now to the Greshams.'

Carrying the black urn as though it was diamonds, Kate came over to the fence and handed it reverently to Julia. 'You've got to make the others drink it, hurry.'

Julia ran with it into the house, so carried away by the solemnness of the occasion that she forgot to worry whether she had been seen. The sound of coughing from the schoolroom told her that Henry was still there and she burst in. 'You've got to drink it.' She flourished the black urn in his face. 'Otherwise Richard won't get his scholarship.'

But Henry shuddered and lay back in his chair, turning away his head. 'I can't, I'd be sick.'

There was no time to argue. 'Traitor,' she shouted at him, and ran up the stairs to Amy.

With bare arms and undressed as far as her flannel petticoat, Amy was standing on her bed, craning over the bars of the window. She turned when Julia came in. 'I wish the apple tree wouldn't get in the way. The fire looks as though it's going out. What have you got there?'

'Drink it,' commanded Julia, 'and wish for the scholarship.'

'I can't, I've just done my teeth.'

With a howl of rage Julia sprang at Amy and would have cuffed her if Amy hadn't jumped out of the way and taken refuge behind the bed. 'You know I can't,' she said virtuously. 'Nobody can eat anything after they've done their teeth. And you mustn't hit me, Papa says you mustn't. Anyway, Kate's calling you.'

In the distance came shouts. 'Where *are* you? Hurry, the fire's going out.'

Julia tumbled downstairs and out again. When she reached the fence she remembered that she had not drunk from the urn yet. Trying to keep her mind fixed on Richard's scholarship and nothing else, she took a mouthful. But it was so unbelievably nasty that all thought of the scholarship was driven from her mind. Not only did it burn and make her eyes water, it was also full of lumps. It needed all her endurance not to spit it out. 'Here,' she said, thrusting it over the fence to Kate.

'You're only just in time. The fire's going out and we've used up all the paper.'

Kate took the urn and carried it back to Richard. Bolder than any of them he put it to his lips and took a deep draught. Then he flung the rest on to the flames, where it sizzled and spurted. 'A libation to the gods!' he called.

Julia and Kate echoed him, but it sounded very flat and unconvincing somehow, and the dying flames just flickered in the charred scraps of paper.

CHAPTER 13

Aunt B Routs the Enemy

The Holly Bank summer term started the next day, the same day, in fact, as the Christ's scholarship examination, though whether or not this was a good omen, Julia could not decide. She had to start the term alone. Until Amy's chicken-pox spots had finally disappeared she would not be going to school. As for Henry, there was no question of his returning to school, though he had long ago been declared free of infection. He just sat over the schoolroom fire in an apathetic way, coughing dismally and looking out listlessly at the bright May sky with its hurrying clouds blown by a sharp east wind.

Amy came racing to meet Julia when she came home that first day. 'I saw Richard going off for the scholarship,' she announced. 'I'm sure he must be ill or something, a cab came to take him to the station and he looked dreadful, all pale and droopy with Mr Holt holding his arm. Do you think he climbed the apple tree and then fell down because of me daring him to, the time we went to tea?' For Amy could not believe that there were people who did not carry out dares.

'Richard doesn't care about dares,' Julia told her scornfully. 'He doesn't mind what people think about him.' She felt a bit guilty as she said this, remembering that if she had not cared so much what the Holts thought, she would not have told all those half-truths yesterday about chicken-pox.

Amy did not see Richard come back from Fareham after the scholarship; in fact they did not see any of the Holts for the next few days, and after the first wonderings about how Richard had got on, they rapidly forgot all about him. Amy had started school by now, and she and Julia were, for once in their lives, in a sort of alliance against Henry. They were both disgusted that they should have to go to school while he sat at home over the fire, having wrecked the holidays (for Julia at least) by driving them into quarantine. They were united in despising him and grumbling about his peevishness.

'I'm sure he could get better if he wanted to; he just doesn't try,' Amy said loudly on the way home from school a week after term had started. They were walking one on each side of Mabel with the prospect of a free afternoon ahead of them because some of the school was rehearsing for the summer concert, in which Amy was too young and Julia too unmusical to take part. But a free afternoon with Henry in his limp convalescent mood was no better than a working one, and both the girls were loud in their complaints about him.

'You'd think he'd try to be cheerful instead of being such a horrible wet-blanket,' said Julia.

'He's low in his spirits. It's only natural,' Mabel said reprovingly. 'He's been really ill, Master Henry has, much iller than you've ever been, Miss Julia. It's taking him a long time to pick up. Why, isn't that the little girl from next door? Looks such an object always, no wonder your pa won't let you play with her. Now come along, Miss Amy, do, don't go loitering and staring like that or we'll have her crossing the road to talk to us.'

But Amy, who could behave like a little street urchin if she chose, had stopped on the kerb and was shouting across the road.

'Was Richard ill on his scholarship day? Why did he go in a fly?'

Kate was by herself, as she nearly always was, and though she must have been on her way back to school after dinner, she was mooching along as though she had nowhere in particular to go. She stopped and stared at Amy over the road.

'Was he ill?' repeated Amy loudly.

'Miss Amy, what ever are you thinking of?' Mabel, scandalized, tugged at her arm. 'That's no way to carry on. Come along at once.'

'I can't hear you,' Kate shouted. 'The wind's making such a noise.' (The wind indeed was very strong and cold today, and was whirling through the bright green new leaves of the plane trees that lined the road and whipping the children's skirts round their shins.)

'Was Richard ill?' bawled Amy, tugging her arm from Mabel and making a cup of her hands. 'Why was he?'

Kate crossed the road. 'Now look at what you've gone and done, Miss Amy,' said Mabel angrily.

'Well,' said Kate when she reached them. 'What's it all about?'

Julia tried to put things on a politer footing. 'How did Richard get on?'

'He hasn't got it, that's what. He was ill. It's all because of you, you and your precious Henry who couldn't even be bothered to come to the sacrifice,' said Kate savagely.

Mabel was indignant. 'However could Master Henry have hurt you? Ever since he got out of bed he's been sitting indoors as good as gold.'

'He wouldn't come out and drink Richard's health. He's been *wanting* him to fail. So's she.' Kate pointed furiously at Amy.

'What a naughty little girl to point,' Mabel said, horrified.

Kate took no notice. 'I asked all the Society to come and only one of you did and that was on the wrong side of the fence. And it's no good saying you had chicken-pox—*I* saw you going to school the day after,' she said accusingly to Julia. 'Then you put frightful things into the libation and made him ill all night.'

Julia was furiously indignant. 'You asked me to get stuff and I did. How did I know he was going to drink it?'

But Amy interrupted. 'Was he sick all night? Too sick to do the scholarship?' she asked, deeply interested.

'Oh he did the exam, but he was ill all the time, too ill to know what he was writing. And there won't ever be another chance, he's too old.'

'Did they tell him he hadn't passed then?' asked Amy.

'They didn't say anything, but how could he have? They'll be sticking up the notice on the school gate this very minute, but his name won't be on it and that's that.'

'Do you think he'll kill himself?' enquired Amy. 'You said he would once.'

'I'm sure he will,' Kate said violently. 'And it'll be all the fault of you Greshams, just remember that.' Pushing Amy roughly out of the way, and without looking where she was going, she ran over the road.

'Well, of all the . . .' Mabel could think of nothing strong enough to say. She just stared outraged at the blue serge figure running violently down the road. 'Miss Amy, I'm downright ashamed of you, I am. You really do say some dreadful things—talking about people killing themselves and all. And shouting like that, nobody would think you came from a nice home.'

'So am I ashamed of her,' Julia shouted. 'Talking like that as if she didn't care whether Richard was alive or dead.' Pushing Amy aside in her turn, she took to her heels and ran, pounding down the road, holding on to her hat with one hand and clutching her school bag in the other. She marched into the house trembling with fury and flung open the schoolroom door.

'Richard's probably failed his scholarship and Kate thinks he'll kill himself. I imagine that you're pleased now.'

'Kill himself?' Henry said feebly.

'The notice about who's passed is on the school gate now. I'm going down to Fareham to see whether he could possibly have passed. It seems to be the only way of stopping him.' This wild idea only flashed into Julia's mind that very moment, she was almost startled to hear what she was saying.

Henry was roused at last. 'Ju, you can't.' His face was ashy pale and he stared at her with wide horrified eyes. 'Not after what happened last time. Girls can't go on trains by themselves.'

'Somebody's got to save Richard, haven't they? And naturally it won't be you. And I don't want to have Richard's death on my conscience even if you don't care.' She was rather pleased with the way this pronouncement came out, it sounded so dramatic and she flung herself out of the room. She was treading stormily up the stairs, very slowly, step by step, inwardly raging at the thought that Amy would soon be in and there was nowhere in the house, nowhere, that she could be by herself alone, when the drawing-room door opened and her mother came out.

'You are home very early, Julia. Where are Amy and Mabel?'

'I ran on, Mamma,' Julia said guiltily. 'They won't be long.'

'You know I don't like you doing that, and just look how hot and untidy you are. Go and make yourself tidy and you can come with me to Mrs Pudney. She was asking about you the other day.'

Tea with Mrs Pudney was not in itself much excitement, but at least it meant that she would be free of the obnoxious presence of Henry and Amy for a little.

By the time Amy came in, she was standing primly by the front door waiting for her mother and looked pointedly the other way as Amy passed.

The tea-party was dull but at least it took her mind off things, and as Mrs Pudney was fond of children she came in for a certain amount of attention, which flattered her. They got back at about five o'clock, but instead of the usual quiet of the house at that time, with homework being done in the schoolroom, and the maids sitting over the kitchen fire the place seemed strangely disturbed.

'Is Master Henry with you, Madam?' said Ellen, rushing instantly to the front door as soon as Mrs Gresham had rung.

'Of course he's not, Mabel. The doctor said he wasn't to go out until it was really warm, certainly not while this wind is blowing.'

'Well, I don't know where he is, Madam, I'm sure. I went upstairs to call him for his tea—he'd been so quiet like, I thought maybe he was asleep in his bedroom because Miss Amy said she hadn't seen him in the schoolroom all afternoon—but there wasn't a sign of him, and we've searched the house up and down and called and called, so I thought perhaps he'd gone with you.' As Mabel paused for breath, Amy came running downstairs.

'I've looked under all the dustsheets in the boxroom,' she said importantly. 'And in the airing cupboard. Oh, I might as well look in the blanket chest in case he's got suffocated there.' She ran off.

'But where *can* he be?' said Mrs Gresham distractedly. 'He's not well enough to go very far, besides, he's not the sort of child just to run off. Could he possibly have gone to those children next door? Julia you'd better go and ask—but mind you apologize for disturbing them.'

Maud opened the door. No, she was sure Henry hadn't come there, she gaped at the very thought of it. All right, she would ask someone if Julia insisted, but it would have to be the master because Miss Holt was out for the day and a lot *he* would know about the children. She kept Julia standing on the doorstep while she went off to the study. She soon came back triumphantly. No, no little boy had been seen here, and Master Richard and Miss Kate were having their tea. She stood at the door staring while Julia went down the path, and she was still staring when Julia turned to shut the gate.

It didn't sound as though Richard was just going to kill himself if he was eating his tea, Julia reflected. And then she knew in a flash where Henry had gone. He had gone to the school gates to look at the notice, and see whether Richard had got a scholarship, and it was all because of what she had said in the heat of the moment, about running off to see for herself. She had not given it another thought, but Henry, goaded on by her taunts, had taken action. She was so busy thinking about this that she hardly paid attention to her mother's questionings when she came back. Mrs Gresham cast round frantically for further possibilities. There was school, perhaps Henry had taken it into his head to slip off to school. It was in the wildest degree unlikely, and anyway, school would be finished for the day, but at any rate it was somewhere to search, and Mabel was ordered to put on her coat and hat and hurry there.

'Can I go too?' Amy demanded. She was enjoying the drama.

'Oh yes, take her, Mabel, only hurry.' Mrs Gresham departed on a further search of the house and more questioning of Ellen, and Julia was left alone. She went into the schoolroom. The fire was nearly dead, a huddle of grey cinders with here and there a dull red flicker as a draught stirred them. She leant her forehead against the brass top of the fireguard and thought. She was as certain as she could be that Henry had gone to Christ's. A lot of the trains from Melsham went through Fareham, it was only twelve miles or so down the line. Their father had two or three times taken them to see the old town and the abbey and the school, so Henry would know the way. But it was no good telling anybody. They would just say 'How do you know?' and there would be endless questioning. Besides, how did she know? She just guessed, and though Henry had never done anything like this before, she knew she was right.

But it was dreadful waiting. Restlessly she wandered out into the hall. The house seemed frighteningly still and lifeless. There was just the ticking of the two grandfather clocks in the dining-room perpetually answering each other, and if she listened hard, the distant murmur of her mother and Ellen talking in the kitchen. She went to the door to hear what they were saying. Ellen was trying to tell Mrs Gresham that Henry was at school, that he was worrying about his schoolwork, but it was clear that she did not believe what she was saying. Julia felt she could bear it no longer, there might be hours and hours of waiting like this; she must do something. She would go down to the station and see whether there was any trace of Henry. Even if they didn't know anything about him at the ticket office, she could find out what trains there were for him to come back on, and she might even get back to the house to find that Henry had turned up after all, from somewhere completely different.

She did not bother to tell anybody, she grabbed her coat and her hat and went out. At first she walked slowly, to fill up the time better but soon she started running, anxious to get to the station, she didn't quite know why. She was breathless when she arrived. Had they seen a boy, she asked at the ticket office, a pale boy of ten. The clerk was gruff, he saw hundreds of boys day in, day out, far too many for his liking, and how could he say which one was pale or rosy, he wasn't a perishing painter. He slammed down the shutter behind his grille.

Julia stood disconsolately in the dirty little waiting room. The people passing through on their way to and from the platform edged round and stared at her curiously, she thought. So she walked over as non-chalantly as she could to examine an ill-printed time-table which was peeling off the boards. It was quite the wrong timetable, not the Fareham one, she saw that at once, but she did not dare move away for fear of being seized by some busybody and questioned. A train came in, people got off it and tramped through the waiting room over the creaking wooden boards. Julia looked over her shoulder to see if Henry was among them. They came past the ticket collector one at a time, and she stared, not with much hope. Then she realized with a jump of horror that she was staring at a hat that she knew, the hat that was waiting to pass the ticket collector now, a brown straw one with two stiff black quills that looked as though they had been torn from an eagle. It could only be Miss Moule's hat, and short-sighted as she was, she could see that Miss Moule had recognized her. It was not pride or courage that made her stand her ground, it was more the horror of the rabbit that has seen a snake. Wordlessly, she and Miss Moule stared at each other over the ticket barrier.

But there was an obstacle before the snake could fall on the rabbit. An elderly, irate man was holding up the stream of passengers while he argued with the ticket collector. He was not only angry, he was also deaf, and the argument was taking a long time, while the passen-gers behind shuffled and muttered impatiently. But still the man argued and she and Miss Moule stared. Another train came in at the far platform. It thundered in and the noise drowned the arguing at the barrier. Perhaps this was why the ticket collector gave up. He stood back, let the elderly man go triumphantly through, and the impatient passengers poured out, as if a bottle had been uncorked.

'At least she can't say I've been reading Lord Byron,' Julia thought as Miss Moule and her eagle feathers advanced on her.

'You are with your parents, I hope,' said Miss Moule, who looked as though she did not believe it for a moment.

'No,' said Julia boldly. 'I am waiting for my brother.' She tossed her head. In fact it was to try to get rid of a piece of hair that was tickling her—she had put on her hat very clumsily and had been running hard—but Miss Moule took it for defiance.

'You are one of the wildest and most hardened children I have ever been unfortunate enough to meet.' Julia looked at a knothole in the dirty floor and rubbed her shoe over it. 'I am thankful my society does not often encounter girls of your hardness even from the worst homes.' Julia lifted her eyes, gave a nervous shrug, and stared past Miss Moule at the ticket collector. To her horror and mortification, who should she see there but Aunt B, flamboyant in bright green and her cheeks redder than ever. Of all the people to witness her disgrace, Aunt B was one of the last she would have chosen. And Aunt B had seen her. 'Coo-ee,' she shouted in a fluting voice and waved. Julia smiled in a sickly way. Miss Moule unfortunately only saw the smile and not the reason for it.

'Will nothing bring home to you the fearful path you are treading?' she said sombrely. Julia lowered her eyes and writhed. She took her eyes off Miss Moule's black reticule and looked nervously at Aunt B again. She was coming through the barrier this minute, but she was pushing in front of her, limp and drooping, the be-draggled figure of Henry, hatless, and in his indoor slippers. Julia gasped. Miss Moule gave an impatient look over her shoulder to see what was distracting Julia's attention, and her glance fell on Henry at once. She swung round and nodded grimly to Aunt B.

'So you have found another of them. I know the parents, and I completely fail to understand how the children can be so wild and reckless. I can only suppose they have wholly unsuitable companions.'

Henry cowered and shrank and clung to Aunt B's arm. He looked utterly exhausted and had black migraine rings all round his eyes. Aunt B tucked his arm through hers and drew herself up.

'If it's my nephew and niece you're referring to, I'll thank you to keep your tongue off them. They're good children though they haven't got a mother and my brother can't keep them as nicely dressed as he'd like.'

'My good woman,' said Miss Moule sharply. 'I have no idea who your niece and nephew may be, but if they are the children I have seen with this little girl, then I suggest they need more control and discipline than they are getting.'

Aunt B's cheerful good humour went. She settled the feather boa round her neck with great ferocity, let go of Henry's arm, put her hands on her hips and leant forward aggressively.

'And who are you a "good-womaning" of, I'd like to know. I'm a dressmaker and not ashamed to own it, but that doesn't mean that I allow myself to be called a woman any more than you would.'

Henry stared at Aunt B with feverish bright eyes. ('Goodness, he must be feeling ill,' Julia thought, 'to stay and look at her like that and not run away.' Henry loved peace so much that whenever possible he took to his heels if he thought there were going to be angry scenes.) Miss Moule, even she, quailed a little in front of Aunt B's flashing eye. But she stood her ground.

'I see no shame in being called woman, since that is what we have been created, for better or for worse,' she remarked haughtily.

'Well, I do see shame, and I'll thank you to keep the word to yourself in future. Now what have you got against my nephew and niece? As far as I know they're having their tea, as good as gold.'

'On this occasion perhaps, since these two children appear to be alone.' Miss Moule eyed Julia and Henry balefully. 'But I have seen them together and I can assert that noise, aggression, defiance, and insolence is what they produce in each other. Though who is the most to blame I cannot say.'

Aunt B put her head on one side and looked at Miss Moule thoughtfully. 'Now I know who you are. You're the person the children call the Old Dame and go nag nag nagging at them all the time till their life's a misery. This little boy's been telling me about it. And what a sour old puss you are to be sure.'

Julia gave a little quiver, half of pleasure, half of horror. Never in all her sheltered life, where even her father's scoldings were conducted in the dressing-room out of earshot of the rest of the house, had she heard this sort of quarrelling in public. She had never realized that grownups had it in them to be so rude to each other, but to carry on like this in the middle of a station with all Melsham to hear!

Miss Moule pressed her lips together tightly. 'I am doing what I believe to be my duty. I am trying to rescue these children from themselves and open their parents' eyes to their behaviour before it is too late.'

'You're doing nothing of the sort,' said Aunt B

robustly. 'You're a nagging old busybody, that's what
you are, always trying to make trouble. There's nothing
wrong with our children at all, they may be a bit noisy,
but that's just healthy. And as for this little boy here, he's
a hero, and I don't care who knows it. He's been down to
Fareham, all the way, just to see whether my nephew's
got his scholarship, and he wasn't feeling any too bright
either—as you can see.' She pushed forward Henry,
reluctant and shrinking, towards Miss Moule.

Miss Moule seemed to be losing ground. 'I don't say
that the children are necessarily evil throughout,' she
began. But Aunt B interrupted her.

'Oh yes you do, and a lot more. Well, you take it
from me that they are not. They're nice good children,

and the trouble with the people that find fault with them is that they haven't got enough to do with themselves alone, and have to go round poking their noses into other people's affairs. Well, we've had enough of it now, go on, be off with you.' And in the face of all Melsham, Aunt B actually flapped her skirts at Miss Moule as though she were a hen or a dog, and Miss Moule turned tail and went without saying another word. Aunt B watched the retreating eagle feathers with triumph.

'Well, there won't be any more trouble there or my name's not Bertha Holt.'

'I think I would like to sit down,' said Henry faintly.

CHAPTER 14

The Gold Medal

Aunt B was very kind. She made Henry sit down on a bench with Julia and went off to find a cab. He just slumped on the bench, leaning heavily against Julia, and said feebly from time to time, 'What will Papa say?'

Julia wondered too. At least he would not hear anything about Henry's escapade until he came back from Scotland, but of course it was dreadful for Henry to have it hanging over his head for so long.

'Did Richard get his scholarship?' she asked suddenly.

Henry's eyes had closed with exhaustion. 'Yes, I suppose so. His name was on the list inside the school gate. Do you suppose Papa will be very angry? Will there be another of those dreadful rows in his dressing-room? I wish I was home, I feel so shivery.'

Aunt B came back with a fly which had just brought some passengers to the station. She bundled the children in and sat talking cheerfully. She seemed to have enormously enjoyed the scene with Miss Moule—'Not that I'm a quarreller myself but some folks just ask for it. Well fancy our Richie getting his scholarship, won't they all just be pleased at home. Mark you, I always said he would, not a moment's doubts did I have. And you going all the way down there, Henry. You needn't have bothered, we'd have heard by post tomorrow. Still, it's nice to know and I'm sure it was very kind of you.'

She chattered on like this the whole way, not seeming to notice how silent the children were. Henry's migraine seemed to be too bad for him to take in anything, but Julia sat rigidly, thinking hard. At first she felt burning with anger that Kate should have talked so wildly about Richard killing himself when all the time he had his scholarship. Then she remembered that it was because she herself had talked so wildly that Henry had run off like this. He had run off to save her getting into worse trouble. It was a heroic thing to do, and, almost in tears, she squeezed Henry's hand gratefully.

But he did not seem to notice. His hand, which was very cold, just lay limply in hers. 'What will Papa say?' he repeated.

'Papa's in Scotland,' Julia reminded him.

'But when he comes back. Mamma's sure to tell him.'

Aunt B patted his knee. 'Don't you worry. Aunt B will deal with that. As soon as your pa gets home I'll come in and tell him the whole story and what a kind little boy you've been for Richard's sake. And if it's that Old Dame of yours you're fretting about, I don't think you'll find her on your doorstep again. Look here, I'll tell you what we'll do. We'll have a really good spready tea to celebrate—the best we've ever had—with everything from Charlwood's that you fancy.'

Henry swallowed. It was plain to Julia that he fancied nothing from Charlwood's at the moment. 'Thank you very much,' he said faintly. Then, while they stood on the doorstep waiting for somebody to answer the bell, he clung to Julia. 'Ju, don't let her come to Papa. It'll make it far worse. She's awfully nice, but she's not Papa's sort of person.'

Ellen came to the door, almost running. She looked dishevelled and worried, and gave a screech when she saw Henry. 'I was just saying to Mabel as it must be the police round to say they'd found Master Henry's corpse. Why, wherever have you been the pair of you? And you, Miss Julia running off too, I just don't know how you could do it. And your ma prostrate, just prostrate, with one of her bad heads on account of you. Just look at you, Master Henry, no hat, your indoor shoes, and you just out of bed. You must have took leave of your senses.'

She drove the two children upstairs. Amy was hanging out of the bedroom door in her nightgown, but they took no notice of her or of her excited questions. In any case, Ellen would not let them stop, she flung open the door of their mother's bedroom and pushed them in.

'Here they are, madam, though where they've been I'm no wiser than you are.'

The curtains were drawn and it was very dark. Julia went a little way in and stumbled over a chair. There was a sigh from the bed.

'Sorry, Mamma,' she said awkwardly. 'And I'm sorry I went away like that. I thought I knew where Henry was so I went to find him.'

'And of course it was too much trouble for you to tell us that you were going to find Master Henry,' said Ellen sarcastically from the door. 'You'd rather have us driven out of our wits than do that. Well, I'll wager those little ragamuffins from next door were at the bottom of it all. I said to Mabel I said . . .'

Mrs Gresham interrupted. 'All right, Ellen. Thank you for having brought them up to me.' Ellen shut the door. Mrs Gresham said in an exhausted voice. 'Is this true? Is this something to do with the Holts?'

Julia's eyes were used to the dimness now, and she could see her mother lying in bed, quite flat with no pillows, and an eau-de-cologne soaked handkerchief on her forehead. She stepped forward eagerly. 'They didn't know about it, Mamma,' she began excitedly. 'He did it quite on his own, it was terribly brave of him . . .'

'Gently, Julia, gently. You know how loud voices hurt my head. Why can't you learn to speak softly?'

Julia tried to lower her voice, but it is difficult to tell a convincing story and win a person over when you are almost whispering. 'He heard that Richard was very worried about his scholarship so he went all the way down to Fareham to see whether he had got it.'

'First Julia, now Henry.' Mrs Gresham seemed to be speaking to herself. 'They seem to have taken leave of their senses. Well, we shall just have to wait for Papa. I can do nothing with you, you are quite beyond my control.'

This sounded terrifyingly like Miss Moule; Julia felt quite sick. 'I'm very sorry I went off too, Mamma.' She forgot to lower her voice in her anxiety to put things right. 'You see, I thought I knew where Henry had gone so I thought I would go down to the station and see if I could meet him or find out something. But it wasn't any good telling you where I was going in case he hadn't gone and you started worrying when you needn't and anyway you couldn't do anything.' She stopped, breathless.

'Oh Julia, do try to show a little more consideration and stop shouting. You had better go now, both of you.'

'But Henry's not very well, Mamma.'

'Ellen will see to him, then. But just go, Julia, please.'

They went, and Julia did not see Henry again that night. She put herself to bed hungry rather than face the scoldings of Ellen and Mabel in the kitchen, and turned her face to the wall, refusing to answer any of Amy's questions.

Their mother did not appear at breakfast next morning, nor did Henry. 'He's ill again,' Ellen told them with a sort of gloomy pleasure. 'It's a judgment on him.'

But in the next few days people rapidly forgot about it being a judgment on him, because Henry was so very ill, more ill than he had ever been. The doctor came first once and then twice a day, the house was hushed and very still, and Mrs Gresham, Mabel, and Ellen took turns at sitting with him, keeping the bronchitis kettle going, lifting him on his pillows. And all the time Henry coughed, a horrible choking cough that made Julia's flesh creep when she heard it. She was not allowed to see him, they said he was hardly conscious, but if you passed his doors you could hear him muttering and moaning. Julia could hardly bear it, she rushed past as quickly as possible. But Amy, who was both tough and curious, reported that Henry was saying over and over again: 'What will Papa say? Will he be very angry? Will he send for me to his dressing-room?'

'They keep on telling him that Papa won't be angry,' Amy said. 'But he just doesn't seem to listen. Isn't it funny?'

But Captain Gresham was not due home for more than a week, and nobody wrote to tell him how ill Henry was. 'No, I am not going to tell him,' said Mrs Gresham when Amy questioned her. 'I don't want to spoil his holiday. Henry will be all right soon. Now run away, and don't bother me, I've quite enough to worry about.'

'Of course, Mamma is afraid of Papa,' Amy announced in the privacy of the schoolroom. 'She's afraid of him being cross because his holiday is spoilt.' The outrageous things that Amy said sometimes had a grain of truth in them, however shocked you might be at first.

But Henry was not getting better, and on Saturday the doctor said he must have a nurse. Amy rushed out and intercepted him just as he was about to get into his brougham. 'I asked him if Henry was so ill that he was going to die,' she told Julia. 'And he looked terribly solemn and said it was in heaven's hands. So I suppose Henry must be almost dying.'

'How can you be so awful?' Julia said violently, and rushed away to the bedroom. There she leant hard against the door so that Amy could not come in. It had never occurred to her that her ideas about early death might work out like this, that Henry would be the dying child and struck down so suddenly. All the romance went; the plumed horses, the thrill of the coffin being carried into the abbey to the sound of solemn music, and she could only think of poor Henry, gasping and coughing in his bedroom and moaning feebly. She darted to her glove drawer and pulled out *Instances of Early Piety* from underneath her handkerchief sachet. Of course the children in there were far more like Henry than anybody else, meek, good, obedient. She held the book close to her eyes and peered at it, at the account of Blessing Fenn aged thirteen who said 'Father, pray for me, that I may have a short and easy passage,' and tears ran down her face so that she could hardly see. She was far too wicked to die herself, but Henry was so good that he easily might. Then she remembered the words 'His heart was as truly great and noble as his high descent' and the tears began to pour faster than ever. Henry had given her those two books, and it was probably a sort of prophecy that he was going to die.

The sound of Amy's footsteps coming up the stairs filled her with panic. She leaned against the door with all her might and tried to rub away her tears on her sleeve. The footsteps stopped outside and Amy pushed at the door.

'Are you there, Julia? I want to come in.' She managed to push open the door an inch or so.

'Well, you can't. Go away and leave me alone.'

'I want to go out. Mamma says I can't unless you come with me.'

'Why ever do you want to go out? Why can't you wait?'

'I want to spend my Saturday money.' Amy pushed harder at the door.

Julia was shocked out of her tears. 'You are the greediest little pig I have ever heard of. Fancy thinking about sweets and your pocket money on a day like this. I suppose you went and plagued Mamma for it?'

'How do you know what I want to spend it on? Oh, do get away from the door, it's my bedroom just as much as yours.' Amy threw herself against the door with a crash. Ellen put her head out of Henry's room.

'For lawks sake, you two, be quiet. Whatever are you up to?'

Dully, Julia stood away from the door and Amy came in. 'Ju, do come with me. I must go out.'

Ju, that was the name Henry called her, Amy scarcely ever used it. Fresh tears came, and to hide them Julia went over to the wardrobe and buried her face among the clothes as she fumbled for her coat. She heard Amy taking coins out of her money-box, the little wooden house inscribed 'Amy's Bank', but she did not turn round.

As they walked down Clifton road, a cab drove past. Amy stared at it. 'That's Henry's nurse, I'm sure. She looked so very tidy. And anyway the cab's stopping at our house, so it must be. Is Henry having a nurse because he's so much worse, or because Mamma's too tired to go on nursing him?'

'I don't know,' said Julia, although she had a pretty good idea that it was the first reason. 'Oh do stop staring and come on.'

They walked towards the shops in Station road in silence. But Amy stopped before they got to Portway's, where they traditionally spent their weekend pocket money. 'I'm going in here,' she announced. 'You can wait for me outside.'

It was Webber's, the toyshop that also sold books of a sort, and had a post office at the far end, and it crossed Julia's mind that perhaps she had misjudged Amy, she might, after all, be going to buy some present for Henry. Only now of course he was far too ill to take any notice.

She waited there, wondering if he would be dead by the time they got back, and wiping away her tears. The bell on the shop door jangled, and Amy came out, looking rather smug and triumphant.

'I've sent a telegram to Papa,' she announced, 'asking him to come home at once.'

Julia always tried hard not to show Amy that she was surprised by anything she did—it was bad for her—but this time she could not help it. She gaped at Amy.

'Did Mamma tell you to?'

Amy looked self-satisfied. 'No, of course she didn't. But I think Papa ought to know and by the time Mamma gets round to it, it may be too late. Anyway, Henry's worrying about him all the time, I'm sure he can't get better till Papa comes.'

'But it'll make him worse. You know how frightened he is of Papa.'

'He won't be angry, I'll ask him not to be,' Amy said arrogantly.

And Julia said nothing to this. In spite of herself, she was impressed and saw depths of wisdom in Amy she had never guessed at. She played with Amy for the whole of the rest of the day, pretending that Mrs Florabella of the doll's house was giving a grand dinner party, and by working harder at the game than she had ever bothered before, she managed to keep both their minds off Henry in his sickroom. But with the night it all came back. She lay awake straining her ears for sounds from his room. The house did not seem to be asleep at all; doors opened and shut, footsteps creaked on the stairs, voices murmured, and from time to time she heard the sound she most dreaded, Henry's coughing, thin and faraway. Perhaps her father would never get Amy's telegram, or perhaps Henry would be dead before he arrived. She put her head under the bedclothes, afraid of waking Amy, and began to cry. Occasionally she put her head out and gasped for air, but she went on crying till she thought her head would burst.

She must have fallen asleep in the end, for she suddenly opened her eyes to find Amy standing on the floor pulling on her clothes. She looked calm and cheerful.

'I expect Papa's having breakfast on the train now. He always catches the same train.' She twisted herself to do up some buttons down her back. 'The thing is, do you think I ought to put on my grey Sunday cashmere, or won't there be anybody to take us to church today?'

Julia was still struggling with her sleepiness and had given no answer when, through the stillness of the house, came the loud ring of the front door bell. 'Papa,' shrieked Amy. 'That must be him already.' Still in her petticoat, with no shoes on, she threw open the door and disappeared. A second or so later, Julia heard her give a shout of 'It *is* Papa!' and go pattering down the stairs.

She was still in her petticoat when Julia, now dressed, went down into the dining-room. Her father had wrapped his travelling coat round her, and she was sitting on his knee, her *déshabillée* unnoticed, while he talked to their mother. He looked anxiously at the door when she came in.

'Oh it's you, Julia. Is Henry awake yet, do you know?' Julia was startled by his appearance. His face was haggard and lined, his shoulders sagging. 'Then he does love Henry,' she thought with astonishment. This had never occurred to her before, Henry and she always seemed to irritate him so much. Before she had time to answer, the nurse put her head through the door. 'You can come now, sir,' she said. And Captain Gresham hastily rose.

By the time he came back Amy was dressed and in the middle of eating her porridge. 'Well,' she said with the proud air of somebody who has put everything right, 'is he all right now?'

But her father's face was as worn and anxious as before. He sat down heavily in his chair, and pushed away his untasted porridge.

'What did he say?' persisted Amy.

'He didn't say anything, my dear. Nurse says he is awake, but he is lying with his back turned to me and he won't open his eyes.'

'That's because he's afraid of you, Papa,' announced Amy in her downright way. But even she was startled at the effect this had. Captain Gresham gave a groan that seemed almost a sob and put one hand over his eyes. 'To be afraid of me, his own father! Too afraid to open his eyes!'

Julia could not bear it. She dropped her spoon with a clatter. 'Papa, it was because you were so angry with me when I went to London. But it's different for a boy, isn't it?' She was almost sobbing herself. 'He's afraid you're going to be very angry with him for running off to Fareham. But, Papa, he did it for Richard's sake, and because of all the horrible things I said to him. I'm far more of a coward than he is, I'm always afraid of what people are going to think. Papa, please, please don't be angry with Henry.' Tears were trickling down her nose now.

Captain Gresham took his hand from his eyes. 'You don't understand. I'm not angry with Henry. But to hear that he is afraid of me—that really is hard to bear.'

Amy stared at him with bright eyes. She did not really understand, but thought her father was still a little angry because of Henry being afraid. 'Oh, but they're all afraid of you except me, Papa. Especially after you were so very angry with Julia. But she only did those things like going to London because she wants to be great—like you said the Greshams ought to be great. I know because she put it in her diary and she always will leave it around so I can't help seeing it, can I? And we made a society with the children next door especially for being great, only we haven't done anything lately because you said we mustn't play with them.'

Amy was chattering briskly on and her father, forgetting for the minute his concern about Henry, was staring at her, bewildered, when there was a ring at the front door. There was a murmur of voices in the hall, then Ellen put her head through the door. She had barely time to say, 'Miss Holt to see you, sir, and she won't take no for an answer,' before Aunt B pushed her way into the room. Richard and Kate, looking rather ill at ease, were behind her.

Aunt B was breathing heavily and was as loudly dressed as ever. 'Captain Gresham is it? Well, pleased to meet you, I'm sure. I saw the cab coming up to the door just as I was getting up our Kate (or trying to get her up, for my word, she's a lazybones in the morning), and I said to myself I'll just step round and have a word with Captain Gresham about young Henry and tell him what a hero he's been. I'm really sorry to hear that he's been poorly.'

Captain Gresham, who had risen to his feet, looked puzzled. 'Henry has been a hero? I'm afraid I don't know the full story. My elder daughter, here, has been telling me some such thing but I don't pretend to understand what it's all about.'

'Why, haven't they told you?' Aunt B was amazed. 'Poor old Henry, he got some idea into his head that Richard wanted to know his scholarship results at once, so off he went chasing to Fareham not even bothering to put on a hat. I got in at Hopton (I'd been down to fit a client there, very difficult figure she has, I'm the only person who understands it), and there was Henry just about all in. But he told me that Richard had got his scholarship (just fancy, our Richard a scholar of

Christ's!). My word, I was pleased—though of course we would have heard by post the next morning. But wasn't it kind of Henry for thinking of it? Such a nice little boy, we're all so fond of him, aren't we, Richard?' Aunt B drew him forward. 'Richard's called here every morning this week, but your maid said little Henry was too ill to see him and everybody else was too busy.'

Richard looked ill at ease and diffident, quite different from his usual air of easy superiority. 'We'd got something for him as a matter of fact. The gold medal of the society we made up—Julia will know about it. It's just that we said we'd give it to the person who was great first and we thought Henry deserved it. It might cheer him up a bit. And my sister is sorry about anything she said that might have upset Julia or Henry. She is prone to speak rather wildly at times.'

'It's the medal from Monarch's new collar that I had for my birthday that we're giving to Henry,' said Kate enthusiastically. 'And do you know, Richard took it to Gaydon Bird the jeweller's and had it engraved specially for Henry.'

She had snatched it from Richard and was just about to show it to Captain Gresham when Mrs Gresham ran into the room.

'Julia, go quickly to Henry. He's sitting up in bed calling you and saying something about a saddle, and Nurse and I can't calm him.'

In a flash Julia knew what it was all about and she was rehearsing comforting words to Henry as she flew up the stairs. But it was difficult to get a word in. Henry with unnaturally glittering eyes in a face that had become frighteningly thin and bony in the last week, was sitting bolt upright in bed, clutching the bedclothes and resisting all the nurse's efforts to make him lie back against his pillows.

'Ju, Ju. I heard Aunt B in the hall. You mustn't let her

see Papa, he'll be so angry. You won't, will you? And the saddle, Kate's got it. You must get it back, they'll be spring cleaning the boxroom any day now. You said you were going to get it back but you never did. Oh do hurry.'

Before Julia had time to say anything her father came striding into the room. 'My poor boy, nobody's angry, how could they be?'

'But the Holts, Papa?' Henry stared at his father with enormous eyes. 'They're in the house, I heard them.'

'And what's wrong with them, pray? Charming people, I wish we'd known them before. That boy says he wants to give you a gold medal for being a hero, or some such thing. The greatest Gresham, eh?'

Henry slept soon after that. 'As quiet as a lamb' the nurse said proudly, as if it was her doing. But he held in one hand the medal from Monarch's collar which said on it, 'Henry Gresham. SAGBOHEICIM medal for Greatness.'

The Holts had gone and everybody felt full of good will. Captain Gresham had actually laughed loudly when Aunt B had announced that she had 'made mince-meat of that Miss Moule' and he told Mrs Gresham that she ought to thank Miss Holt for banishing a bogey that had worried her for years. But what touched him most was the sight of Kate staggering in with the saddle polished as it had never been polished before, with stirrups burnished like silver. He even told her to take it back and borrow it for a bit longer, it could not be in better hands.

Amy was quick to take advantage of her father's softened mood. She sat on his knee and smoothed his moustaches with her finger. 'Then can we always play with the Holts? Always whenever we want, do you promise? I don't want to play with *them* so very much, but their tree is very good to climb, and they've got a wonderful shed'

'I had to make him promise,' she told Julia afterwards. 'You can never be *quite* sure with Papa, he does change his mind sometimes and roar. But I don't think he'll ever roar at Henry again. Still, if only you asked him about the Holts when they first came I'm sure it would have been all right. Or I could have asked for you'

And Julia, who had developed a surprising respect for Amy's judgment, did not spring at her and shake her as she once would have done.

The Moon of Gomrath

ALAN GARNER

Colin and Susan turned. The flames were a scarlet curtain between hill and sky, and within them, and a part of them, were three men. Even while the children looked, they became more solid, rounded, and independent of the flames through which they stared. Then they were real, and terrible . . . Red were they all, weapons and clothing and hair, both horses and men. The three horsemen rode slowly out of the fire.

'Run,' said Colin to Susan.

But they were not half-way to the trees before there was a drumming of hoofs, a flutter of cloaks, and Colin and Susan were hooked off their feet and thrown across the necks of horses that hurled themselves through the night as though world's ruin were at their heels.

The Weirdstone of Brisingamen, Elidor, and *The Owl Service* are also in Lions.

Ghostly Experiences

CHOSEN BY SUSAN DICKINSON

The remarkable revival of interest in ghost stories at the present time is curious, for ghost stories traditionally belong to that great age of story telling: the 19th century. And yet, despite the distractions of the television screen, ghost stories are much in demand particularly among the young. Here you will find examples of ghost stories ranging from R. L. Stevenson and J. S. LeFanu in the 19th century to the most contemporary of contemporary writers – Alan Garner and Joan Aiken.

Some of the stories are truly spine-chillers; some of the ghosts are gentle, some are not; but the collection should provide plenty of ghostly 'pleasure'.

'A splendid collection of supernatural adventures.'

New Statesman

'The stories in this collection have been chosen with discrimination and illustrated with a sure intuition.'

Growing Point

Thursday's Child

Noel Streatfeild

'Noel Streatfeild's position in the children's book world is unique. She has had all the accolades: a Carnegie Medal, a Bodley Head Monograph—and both critical and popular esteem . . . She is endlessly inventive, full of verve and real understanding of the surfaces of childhood.'

Times Literary Supplement

'The past comes to life with humour and grace in *Thursday's Child*, a period piece set at the turn of the century. Margaret Thursday makes a splendid heroine . . . A whole way of life springs brilliantly to life.' *Growing Point*

'Authenticity blends beautifully with romance . . . Children will love it.' *Daily Telegraph*

Thursday's Child 'promises to be a minor classic and it is enchantingly and appropriately illustrated by Peggy Fortnum.'

Birmingham Post

Charley

JOAN G. ROBINSON

'I don't want Charley. You know that . . .'

So Auntie Louie didn't want her, nor did Aunt Emm. Well, she could do without them, too.

So Charley runs away to live in a field. Her bed is a bit hard and there are earwigs in her supper, but the henhouse is familiar and comforting. She decides she is going to be all right until the sun goes down . . . Perhaps she *should* move closer to Aunt Louie's house just in case of an earthquake or a deluge . . .

Charley's week in the woods is a mixture of joy and terror, magic and misery, and from it all she gains a new understanding of herself and those she thought didn't love her.

When Marnie Was There by Joan G. Robinson is also in Lions.

The Sword in the Stone

T. H. WHITE

Probably only the magician, Merlyn, knew that his pupil, the Wart (to rhyme with 'Art') would one day be the great King Arthur.

For six years Merlyn was the boy's tutor and the Wart learned all manner of useful things; such as what it is like to be a fish or a hawk or a badger.

Then the king, Pendragon, died without heirs. And King Pellinore arrived at the court with an extraordinary story of a sword stuck in an anvil stuck to a stone outside a church in London. Written on the sword in gold letters were the words

> *Whoso Pulleth Out This Sword of*
> *This Stone and Anvil, is Rightwise*
> *King Born of All England.*

The last person anybody expected to pull out the sword was the Wart but then he had had Merlyn as his tutor for the past six years.

The Donkey Rustlers

GERALD DURRELL

This lively story with a Greek island setting tells how Amanda and David plot to outwit the unpleasant local mayor and help their Greek friend, Yani. The villagers, and especially the mayor, depend on their donkeys for transport. If the children are to blackmail them successfully the donkeys must disappear – and disappear they do, to the consternation of the whole village . . .

Told in Gerald Durrell's dashing style with his own particular brand of humour, this story will be eagerly read by older children.